MIDSUMMER MAGIC

Fearing that her ex-husband plans to take their daughter away with him to New Zealand, Lauren escapes with little Amy to the remote Cornish cottage bequeathed to her by her Great-aunt Hilda. But Lauren had not even been aware of Hilda's existence until now, so why was the house left to her and not local school-teacher Adam Poldean, who seemed to be Hilda's only friend? Lauren sets out to learn the answers — and finds herself becoming attracted to the handsome Adam as well.

REBECCA BENNETT

MIDSUMMER MAGIC

Complete and Unabridged

LINFORD
Leicester

First published in Great Britain in 2017

First Linford Edition
published 2017

*A catalogue record for this book is available
from the British Library.*

ISBN 978–1–4448–3254–9

Published by
F. A. Thorpe (Publishing)
Anstey, Leicestershire

Set by Words & Graphics Ltd.
Anstey, Leicestershire
Printed and bound in Great Britain by
T. J. International Ltd., Padstow, Cornwall

This book is printed on acid-free paper

1

The sound of the sea puzzled her when she woke, sunshine dazzling her eyes. Stiffly, she moved her head away from the car window. And then she remembered.

The letter.

Driving, panic-stricken, for what seemed like the whole day, with Amy bewildered and fretful on the rear seat.

Amy!

Lauren twisted round, seeing the partially open door, the crumpled blanket trailing from it to the ground.

Her fingers knotted together, knuckles whitening. Had Duncan found them so soon? Surely it wasn't possible. How could he? There was no way ...

She was running, running. Through the neglected garden of the old house, along a worn brick path bordered with a straggle of lavender and lemon balm. Sharp, throat-catching fragrance enveloped her as she brushed past dew-wet trailing leaves.

Below, in the cove, she could see a small boat swaying in shallow water. A man held the side with one hand. Beside him, Amy stood, ankle deep.

There were steps leading down to the beach, cut into the granite of the shallow cliff. Six, maybe seven. Lauren didn't bother to count. Her trainers slithered on the wet stone. Sand, damp from the outgoing tide, dragged at her feet as if desperate to hold her back.

'Amy!' Fear, turned now into fury, made Lauren's voice strident.

Both heads turned. Both faces smiled. But Lauren didn't notice their smiles; only the amazing colour of the man's eyes. Like the sea on a cloudless summer's day.

'How dare you take my child!' she blazed, catching Amy's hand tightly in her own as she glared up at him.

Trying to hold the boat steady, he answered her calmly. 'It's OK. She's fine. I saw her coming down the steps when

I was out there fishing. Unless you live here, you wouldn't know, but there's a very strong current off this part of the coast. By the time I got back here, she was happily wading along the edge.'

Without listening to his explanation, Lauren was already hurrying back across the sand, the little girl scampering along next to her. 'You must never, never talk to strangers, Amy. I've told you that so many times, haven't I?'

'But he's a nice man, Mummy. And he's caught a fish. We were going to bring it for you to cook for breakfast.'

Breakfast, Lauren thought ruefully. First she had to go back into that house, and the idea filled her with dread.

Once she'd turned the key, the front door creaked open reluctantly into a narrow hallway. At one end was the kitchen, its salt-hazed window looking out over the cove; and through it, Lauren saw the man in his boat, fishing a little way off the shore.

'Are you going to make breakfast now, Mummy?'

3

Lauren eyed the black range set into one wall. With the power cut off, there didn't seem to be any other means of cooking. A small whistling kettle rested on the top. Until she could get that thing working, she couldn't even make a cup of tea. Not that she'd brought any food with them. In her frantic haste to get away, there hadn't been time.

'We'll have to buy something for us to eat first, sweetheart. I think we passed a shop down in the village when we were on the way here. Let's go and find it, shall we?'

Whether it was the damp from its night by the sea, she didn't know, but no way could Lauren get the car to start.

'Never mind, darling,' she said, trying not to let Amy see her growing desperation. 'We'll just have to walk there.'

It didn't seem so far when she'd been driving. Now the narrow lane was endless, winding its way down between steep grassy banks where white heads of cow parsley intermingled with tall pink spikes of foxgloves and a scattering of bluebells,

4

to sway lazily in the wind.

After passing a cottage, thatch-roofed, with whitewashed bulging stone walls, round the next corner she saw, to her relief, a small shop that, from the variety of items in its window and piled up outside, appeared to sell everything.

'Staying up in old Miss Trevaunance's house, are you, m'dear?' the woman behind the counter enquired. 'My Ted said he saw a car drive up there late last night, when he was out walking the dog.'

Moving a heap of newspapers to one side, she continued, 'Desolate place that can be, come a storm, and we do get some nasty vicious ones at times. Don't know how she took it on her own all those years. Independent, though. Right up to the end. Just drifted away in her sleep, she did. Lovely way to go.'

She smiled at Lauren. 'Still, you'll probably be knowing all about that, I dare say.'

'I didn't even realise my great-aunt existed under a few weeks ago, Mrs...' Lauren hesitated.

'Mrs Quin, m'dear. Your great-aunt,

was she? And you never knew her? Well, there's a surprise. One carton of milk? Best make it two. Without a fridge it won't keep long, you know. Not at this time of year. Anything else, was there?'

'Oh, matches. Several boxes, please. The power is off, and there's only a rather ancient stove.'

Mrs Quin laughed. 'Wouldn't have nothing modern, would Miss Trevaunance. Now, how about some of these potatoes? Dug yesterday, they were. All local. Lovely flavour. Just wash them under the tap. Don't need no scraping.'

By the time she'd finished, Lauren eyed the growing pile on the counter with dismay.

'Don't you fret about carrying this lot home, m'dear. I'll have my Ted bring it up later on this morning. Do him good to stir his stumps. You take what you need for your dinner, and he'll have the rest there before you've eaten it. Now, my little love,' she said, bending over the counter to Amy, 'ask your mummy if you can have one of my home-baked gingerbread men, for being such a good girl while she's been giving her order.'

'And you can choose some sweets, Amy. See, in those jars along there,' Lauren said, pointing.

When the child was engrossed, she quietly asked Mrs Quin, 'There was a man fishing out in the cove — thirtyish, dark hair ... blue eyes.'

'That'll be young Adam Poldean. Schoolmaster here, he is. Lives in that little thatched cottage halfway up the hill. You'll have passed it on your way here. Usually fishes from that point, does Adam. Favourite place of his.'

Oh, is it, Lauren thought grimly, and, adding Amy's sweets to the carrier bag of groceries she was taking with her, said goodbye.

Adam Poldean, Mrs Quin's words echoed in Lauren's head as she began to climb the hill, with Amy skipping along beside her. The name had a Cornish lilt to it. She remembered the thick darkness of his hair and deeply tanned skin of his face and arms. Were all Cornishmen like that? And were their eyes always so blue?

Seeing the pale thatch of the cottage, part-hidden by pearly white blossom overhanging a pink thrift-covered wall, she quickened her step. Taking Amy's hand in hers, she crossed to the other side of the road. No way did she want to meet that man again.

'I'm a seagull, Mummy,' Amy sang. 'Look at me flying.' She raised her thin arms in the air and waved them up and down, her head turning to make sure Lauren was watching, her feet suddenly tangling together. Her shriek as she tumbled onto the stony ground far out-rivalled those of the white birds circling high above the cliffs.

'Oh, Amy!' Lauren cried, bending to pick her up.

'It's bleeding, Mummy!' Amy sobbed, staring down at a bright bead of colour slowly trickling from one knee.

'Well, we can't have that, can we?' a deep voice startled Lauren, and she spun round to see the tall figure of Adam Poldean advancing towards them.

Without another word, he swung Amy into his arms and carried her down the gravel path to the open door of the white-washed cottage.

And Lauren had little choice but to follow.

2

As Lauren reached the front step, the smell of coffee drifted towards her, and her empty stomach churned.

Bending his head to enter the doorway, Adam Poldean strode on into the kitchen and sat Amy carefully on the wooden draining-board beside the sink. 'Now,' he said, smiling at the little girl, then glancing up at Lauren, 'if your mummy will allow me, let's see what damage you've done.'

Amy's tear-wet eyes gazed anxiously back at him, her bottom lip quivering. 'Will all my blood run out?' she sobbed.

Adam pursed his lips and studied the knee thoughtfully. 'Just enough to cover one petal of a daisy, I should say.' He lifted a square first-aid box down from an overhead cupboard.

Lauren watched him pour warm water into a small dish, then add a few drops of antiseptic.

'If you look through the window behind you, Amy, you might see some kittens.'

The child's head turned swiftly.

'Over there. Under that tree.' His fingers were deftly bathing the wound as he spoke, removing tiny bits of gravel. 'There should be three of them.'

'In a funny sort of basket?' Amy enquired, her gaze intent on the garden.

'That's right.' He undid a strip of plaster and pressed it firmly over the graze. 'Do you want to go out there and play with them?'

Amy's mouth widened into a smile, and then she shot Lauren a cautious glance. 'Can I, Mummy?'

Lauren nodded silently.

When the little girl had disappeared into the garden, her knee forgotten in the excitement of playing with the kittens, Adam Poldean gave Lauren a quizzical look. 'I hope you didn't object too strongly to me talking to your daughter this time?'

Lauren felt colour burn into her cheeks. 'No,' she said, and couldn't prevent her earlier anger from rekindling. 'But I would've thought you of all people would realise just how dangerous it is to encourage a child to speak to a stranger, like you did on the beach this morning.'

His dark eyebrows lifted a fraction. 'Me of all people?' he queried.

'You are a schoolmaster, aren't you? The lady in the shop said… ' Lauren's voice faltered as she caught the full force of his brilliant blue eyes.

'So you've been checking up on me with Mrs Quin.'

Annoyance prickled through Lauren at his shrewd comment. 'Well, one can't be too careful nowadays,' she retorted.

The amusement died from his eyes. 'No,' he agreed, 'you can't. And that's a very sad thing.' He rinsed the dish and returned the first-aid box to its shelf. 'Am I allowed to say something in my defence, though?'

'That you're a teacher and therefore exempt?'

'No,' he replied, leaning his long back against the edge of the sink and regarding her steadily. 'But when I see a small child in imminent danger from the sea, as Amy was this morning, I react swiftly.'

Lauren bit her lower lip.

'There was quite obviously no one with her,' he went on relentlessly.

Interrupting him, Lauren said, 'We had to sleep in the car. It had been a long journey down here from London. And then ... ' She swallowed and took a deep breath. 'When I eventually found the place, the whole house was in darkness. No power on. Nothing. All I could do was wrap Amy in a blanket and take her back to the car. It wasn't how I'd expected to be spending the night.'

Her teeth clenched over her lip again, refusing to let this man see how near she was to tears. 'When I woke up and found her gone ... and saw you with her on the beach ... I just... '

His stern gaze softened slightly. 'I'm sorry, but seeing her on her own like that, I brought the boat back to shore and enticed her out of the water, with the promise of one of the mackerel I'd caught.' Levering himself away from the sink, he picked up the percolator. 'Have you had any breakfast yet?'

The abrupt change in his conversation surprised Lauren, and she shook her head.

His mouth tilted at the corners. 'Expecting the milkman to deliver, were you? And bring half a dozen eggs?'

Her chin rose. 'I hadn't ever seen the house until we arrived last night.'

'And didn't realise it was at the world's end?'

'No,' she admitted, savouring the smell of coffee as he poured two mugs.

'Are you renting it, or what?' he asked, taking a jug of milk from the fridge and passing it across the table towards her.

'It's mine. My Aunt Hilda ... well, Great-aunt Hilda as she really was, left it to me when she died.'

'So you're Lauren?'

She gave him a perplexed glance over the rim of her mug. 'How do you know that?'

'Your great-aunt talked about you frequently.'

'Talked about me?'

'Almost constantly, towards the end.'

'But she didn't know me. I'd never met her, or even heard of her. I had no idea who she was when I received the solicitor's letter with the deeds of the house and some keys a few weeks ago.'

Adam produced a crusty loaf from a cupboard and began to slice it thickly. 'Toast?'

Lauren's stomach groaned, and she saw him grin as he put two slices into a toaster.

'That's rather strange, because your great-aunt had albums of photographs of you.'

'Are you sure it was me?'

'Definitely. All neatly labelled 'Lauren'. As a baby, chubby little toddler, and onwards until you were rather a skinny teenager.' He dropped a slice of hot toast onto a plate and passed it to her. 'You've certainly changed a bit since then.'

'But why …?'

His blue eyes danced. 'Do you really want me to tell you?'

Colour flooded her cheeks. 'I mean, how did Aunt Hilda have photos of me? Where did she get them? Did she ever say?'

Adam opened the fridge again and took out a dish of butter. 'You'd better start on that toast before it gets cold,' he suggested. 'There's marmalade in the glass dish, if you'd like some. I can thoroughly recommend it. Mrs Quin's sister made it. Do you mind if I join you? Hot buttered toast is rather a weakness of mine.'

Lauren waited, impatient for him to continue, while he pulled out a chair, sat down, and spread butter thickly on another slice.

'I've no idea where the photos came from, but your great-aunt definitely had them. She showed them to me many times. They were her pride and joy.'

His strong white teeth bit deeply into the marmalade, and Lauren watched his mouth move as he crunched the toast. 'Aren't the albums still up there in the house?'

'Like I said, we only arrived last night.

16

Everywhere was in darkness,' Lauren replied. 'I haven't even had time to look round the place or do anything yet — and I needed to buy some food. When we get back there, I shall have to find out how to make the kitchen range work. All the electricity is turned off.'

Adam laughed, and Lauren saw his wide mouth curl at the corners into well-used lines. 'Ah, yes. That old range would prove a problem. I think your great-aunt was the only one who could master it. Nothing and no one would dare to do otherwise with Miss Trevaunance. She could be quite a dragon.' He looked thoughtfully across at Lauren. 'You probably take after her.'

'Mummy!' Amy's alarmed face appeared in the kitchen doorway before Lauren could make an indignant reply. 'Those baby kittens are *eating* the mother cat.'

Adam's eyebrows slanted upwards and he gave Lauren a mischievous glance. 'Perhaps now is the time for you to give your daughter a biology lesson.'

She smiled back at him. 'Oh no, Mr Poldean. As a schoolteacher, I'm sure you're able to explain such things far better than I can.'

'OK then, Amy,' he said, quite unperturbed as he rose to his feet and took the child's small hand in his. 'Let's go and see those kittens have their breakfast, shall we?'

Lauren remained in the kitchen, finishing her coffee. Through the window she could see Adam's dark head bent low beside Amy's fair one. The murmur of their voices floated back to her, but their words were too faint for her to hear. Knowing the complexity of her daughter's questions, Lauren wondered just how well Adam was coping.

Her gaze roved round the kitchen, surprised by its tidiness. Apart from the crockery they were using, everything was neatly stowed away in overhead cupboards. No dirty saucepans or dishes lay anywhere. Every surface was clear — and clean. Adam Poldean was obviously a very domesticated man, she decided,

18

licking a trace of marmalade from her fingers before she put her empty plate into the white porcelain sink.

A door slammed, creating a flurry of sound in the hallway behind her. Lauren turned. Coming into the kitchen was a young woman in a billowy cotton dress swirling with flame-coloured flowers. She was tall, pretty, suntanned — and heavily pregnant.

When she saw Lauren, she smiled. 'Hi!' she said, holding out a slender hand. 'I'm Kate.' She lowered the basket she was carrying onto the kitchen table, and Lauren saw that it brimmed with strawberries. 'Would you like some? One of our friends has a garden overflowing with them. Adam and I will never get through all these. They're not quite the same when you freeze them, are they? And as for making jam — I'd be hopeless.'

Without waiting for an answer, the woman rummaged in one of the cupboards, produced a plastic box, and swiftly filled it. 'There! They'll be gorgeous with a dollop of clotted cream.'

She popped one into her mouth and held out another luscious berry to Lauren. 'Are you on holiday down here?'

Her voice was low and rather throaty. The kind a man would find attractive, Lauren decided. But then, Kate was a very attractive woman. Her tanned skin glowed with a soft peachy bloom.

Lauren felt a twinge of envy, remembering those never-ending months when she was pregnant with Amy and felt constantly drained of energy. Or was it because of Duncan? she reflected. He was on his second, or maybe third, affair in the eighteen months they'd been married by then.

'Is that your little girl out there with Adam?' Kate interrupted Lauren's thoughts. 'She looks adorable. How old is she? Three? Four? I hope that's what we'll have, a girl. I could've been told our baby's sex when I had my scan, but that would take all the excitement out of things, don't you think? Rather like opening all your Christmas or birthday presents before the actual day. I really don't know how people can do that, can you? I just love surprises.'

She wrinkled up her nose in thought. 'I suppose it does help if you want to paint the nursery pink or blue, or buy the right sort of clothes, though. Did you know what you were having?'

Lauren nodded, feeling almost breathless trying to keep up with the other woman's rapid conversation. 'Duncan — he was my husband — insisted we were told.' She hesitated before going on ruefully, 'He was like that.'

'Was?'

'We're divorced,' Lauren said abruptly.

'Oh, I'm so sorry. Adam always says I speak first and think afterwards. He's quite right, of course. He always is.'

'I'm sorry, too.'

Kate's hazel eyes stared questioningly back at her. 'You still love him? Didn't you want the divorce?'

Lauren shook her head. 'But I didn't have a great deal of choice. Duncan met someone else while I was pregnant, and she decided it was to be marriage or nothing.' She felt the gentle touch of the woman's's fingers on her wrist.

'That's so awful,' Kate murmured. 'It must be terrible if you love someone, and then... ' She glanced out of the window to where Adam and Amy were crouched over the kittens' basket. 'I don't think I could bear that.' Turning back to Lauren, she asked, 'Has your ex married her, or might you get back together again?'

'The wedding was two months ago.' Lauren paused, then continued, 'Amy was bridesmaid.' Her vision suddenly blurred with tears. 'I wasn't even there to see her. All I saw were the photos. She was so pretty in a forget-me-not blue dress and circlet of tiny flowers on her head. And now ...' Lauren breathed in deeply. 'And now, Duncan and his new wife Naomi want her to live with them. He's been offered a job in New Zealand. They say she'll have a far better life in a family — Naomi has a boy and girl from her first marriage — than on her own living with me. And I know it's probably true.'

Brushing her hand across her eyes, she stood up quickly. 'We must be getting back. Until I've beaten Aunt Hilda's kitchen range into submission, I can't even cook a meal.'

'Oh, Adam will come and give you a hand. I'll call him.'

'No!' The word burst out. 'There's no need. The sooner I learn to cope with the wretched thing, the easier it will be.'

Picking up the plastic box, Kate said, 'Don't forget the strawberries.'

Amy ran in through the door, her heart-shaped face glowing with excitement. 'Adam says I can have one of those kittens when they're big enough.'

'If ... ' Adam prompted, following her into the kitchen.

'If you let me,' Amy added reluctantly. 'You will, won't you, Mummy? Please?'

'I see you've met Kate, so I don't need to introduce you,' Adam said, picking up his half-cold mug of coffee and, with a grimace, spooning away the skin that had formed on its surface. 'Did you manage to get a word in edgeways? I never do.'

'Adam!' Kate protested with a laugh, and aimed a mock blow at his chin.

'Can I have a kitten, Mummy?'

'We'll see,' Lauren replied, carefully placing the strawberries in the top of her carrier bag. 'Have you said thank-you to Mr Poldean for mending your knee?'

The little girl shot a surprised glance down at her leg and grinned. 'I'd forgotten it was hurting.' She chuckled. 'Thank you, Adam. Please may I eat one of those strawberries now?'

★　★　★

The sun was high by the time they reached Aunt Hilda's cottage. Below it, the sea glinted like myriad stars fallen from the night sky.

'Can I go and make sandcastles?' Amy pleaded once they were indoors and the shopping stowed away in one of the cupboards.

'Not on your own,' Lauren replied firmly.

'Why not?'

'Because it's far too dangerous. The sea comes right up the cliff when the tide's in. You can play in the garden, but no further. Will you promise me, Amy? No going down the steps.'

'If the sea did come right up, I could swim,' the little girl said, nibbling one of the strawberries as she looked up from under her thick lashes at Lauren.

'Of course you couldn't, Amy.'

'If I tried I could.'

'Well, you mustn't try. Not without me with you. There are currents out there that would sweep you away, and I'd never see you again.'

'Currants?' Amy said, her forehead puckering into a frown. 'Like in buns?'

'No, sweetheart!'

'Adam's going to teach me to swim. All the children in his school have to learn. He told me. And I can go to his school, 'cause there's a nursery one, like I went to with Mark and Andy when we lived with Aunty Liz.'

Lauren looked doubtfully at her daughter's upturned face. Amy's imagination was very fertile.

'Adam did say he'd teach me to swim, Mummy,' Amy insisted, reading Lauren's expression. 'And how to catch fishes. And make ginormous sandcastles. And let me have one of his kittens. They have to be big enough to eat things all by themselves first, though.' Her brown eyes widened. 'Did you know that mummy cats keep milk inside them? They've got little wobbly things on their tummies for the baby kittens to suck it out. Adam told me. He knows everything. I'll go and pick some flowers if you like.'

'Only in the garden, Amy,' Lauren warned. 'You won't go down those steps to the beach, will you?'

It's going to be a worry having the sea so near, she thought. *And the threat of Duncan and Naomi just waiting to find a reason to take her away from me.*

3

At one o'clock Lauren was still trying to light a fire in the kitchen range. Before it went out each time, choking smoke billowed out, swirling upwards to lose itself among thick cobwebs hanging from the ceiling.

The whole place needs a good clean, Lauren decided, her gaze roaming over whitewashed walls that flaked in patches where damp had crept in around the window frame. *What will it be like here in a winter gale?* she wondered, recalling Mrs Quin's ominous words in the shop earlier that morning.

Salt hazed the window, making it difficult to see out to where the cliff curved like a horseshoe encircling the cove. In the sunshine, it looked beautiful. Seabirds dipped low on silent wings, appearing to hang motionless before settling on some tiny crevice in the sheer face of the granite. Waves curled in across the pale sand, white-crested, and then as swiftly retreated, leaving it a darker shade of gold edged with a delicate feathering of seaweed. Others rose high over jagged rocks, wisping into mist before vanishing.

It was a view Lauren could have gazed at all day. Soothing. Restful. A view she knew would be ever-changing, and yet remain the same. A view that had been there for centuries. A view that her great-aunt had lived with for most of her life.

And has bequeathed to me, Lauren thought. Someone she'd never even met.

'All for you.'

Amy's voice, as she danced into the kitchen clutching a handful of bluebells and pink campion, startled her. It was as if they were Aunt Hilda's words.

'I'll find a vase, Mummy.'

The child was gone again, moving like quicksilver, and seconds later returned slowly, carrying a cut-glass vase. 'There's a magic boat in the other room,' she said, her voice breathless with excitement. 'All made of rainbows. Come and see.' She placed the vase carefully on the table and caught hold of Lauren's hand, tugging it gently.

Lauren had only glimpsed the living room, shadowy and dark, the previous night. Now it blazed with sunshine.

'Look, Mummy!' Amy ran across the room and knelt on the faded chintz-covered window seat to lean against the sill, her chin cupped in her hands, her expression filled with wonder.

In the centre of the windowsill rested a three-masted glass galleon, the sun's rays glinting on every miniature sail to produce myriad vivid rainbows. Splinters of colour shimmered away in every direction, turning the ship into a fairy-tale creation.

'It *is* magic, isn't it, Mummy?' Amy's voice was merely a whisper, her gaze fixed on the iridescent glass. 'So I can make a wish, can't I?'

As Lauren watched, the child's eyes closed, her small mouth forming silent words. Then her eyelids flew open, and a smile curved her lips.

'What did you wish?' Lauren asked, her curiosity roused by the look on her daughter's face.

The smile deepened, dimpling Amy's cheeks. 'It's a secret.' One finger hesitantly touched the tiny glass pennant flying from the mast. 'But I can tell you 'cause you're my mummy, and you have to tell mummies everything.'

Small face upturned, she looked at Lauren. 'I heard you tell Aunty Liz when we were staying with her that nobody wanted us anymore. So I wished that somebody did want us. Now I'm going to wish it every day until it comes true.'

Her brown eyes, full of trust, were turned to Lauren. 'It *will* come true now, won't it? 'Cause this is a magic ship.'

Lauren felt her throat tighten with sudden pain. How could one destroy such implicit faith?

A rap of sound from the front door knocker made her spin round, and through the window she saw the tall figure of Adam Poldean leaning against the side of the porch, his hair tousled by the sea breeze.

'I'll go and open the door for you, Mummy,' Amy shrieked, jumping down from the window seat and running into the hallway.

Lauren followed more slowly. Adam Poldean seemed to appear rather too frequently for her liking.

'Kate sent me up with a pot of cream to go with those strawberries — or have you eaten them already?' His height filled the doorway, his dark head lowered a fraction so that he could speak to her.

'No, not yet.' Hesitating for a moment, Lauren continued, 'We haven't had our lunch yet.'

She saw amusement creep into his eyes. 'Having trouble with that kitchen range?' he enquired, brushing a finger lightly across her cheek and holding it up black with soot.

Before she could reply, he had crossed the hall and was striding into the kitchen. 'It can be a bit of a pig at times,' he confided, lifting the round lid and letting a cloud of dense smoke gush out, to billow chokingly round them.

'Oh no!' Lauren cried out, coughing as she backed away. 'Look what you've done.'

'Look what *you've* done,' he retorted, extracting a smouldering wodge. 'What's all this damp paper doing in here?'

'I found a pile in the shed near the coal. Nothing else would make it light,' she replied defensively.

'Neither will this. Not when it's soggy. No wonder there's so much smoke. I'll have to start from scratch and remove this lot.'

'You'll get filthy.'

'I can always go for a swim afterwards.' He knelt down in front of the range and began to dismantle it. 'Don't look so distraught, Lauren. It will light, I promise you. And once it has, all you have to do is keep it going.' He rubbed one hand across his nose, leaving a dark smudge. 'Why don't you take Amy down to the beach and leave this brute to me?'

Too tired and worn out to argue,

Lauren followed his suggestion.

By the time Adam called them, she was beginning to enjoy herself. Amy insisted that they both paddle; and as they swished along in the shallow water, with sunshine warming the nape of her neck, Lauren felt the tension of the past few days begin to slip away.

It really is a beautiful place to be, she decided, watching the clear water thicken with swirls of sand as her feet moved. And her thoughts turned once more to Great-aunt Hilda. *What was she like?* Lauren wondered. *And why has nothing ever changed in that house? It's like living in a time warp. Everything is as it was seventy or more years ago.*

But I shall get to know her, Lauren silently vowed. *Given time. Every single item in the house holds a clue to its owner. Like the glass galleon on the windowsill that catches the sunshine, turning it into magical rainbows.*

'You can come back indoors now, Lauren. It's quite safe,' Adam's voice spoke quietly from behind her, and she turned to meet his smile.

'You've actually made that thing work?' she asked, wading out of the shallows and feeling the grit of sand under her wet toes.

'Glowing like a furnace, and the oven waiting for whatever you're going to cook in it.'

'Mrs Quin suggested I take some pasties that her sister had made.'

'Ideal. Especially if followed by strawberries — and clotted cream.'

'Thank you for bringing it.'

'You've Kate to thank for that.' He fell into step beside her while Amy skipped on ahead, patterning the sand with tiny footprints.

'When's the baby due?' Lauren asked.

'Any time now.'

'Kate's hoping for a girl, isn't she? How about you?'

'Me?' His dark eyebrows rose and he shrugged. 'It doesn't really concern me.'

She frowned. 'Well, it should.'

He picked up a flat grey stone and skimmed it across the incoming waves. Lauren saw it bounce once, twice, three times before disappearing.

'I don't see why. It's Kate's baby.'

'You're rather offhand about it all, aren't you?'

'Am I?' he said, gazing down into her eyes. 'To be honest, I haven't given the baby a great deal of thought. I'm sure I'll enjoy seeing it on occasion, though.'

Lauren's bare toes dug into the sand as she stopped walking to glare at him. 'On occasion? That doesn't sound very caring. I thought your main concern was children.'

'I teach them, if that's what you mean. Anyway, I very much doubt I shall be seeing this baby very often.'

'Not very often? What sort of father does that make you?'

'When the time comes, a very good one, I hope.' He stood aside, waiting for Lauren to climb the cliff steps, but her hand gripped the wooden rail and she remained there, unmoving.

'Is that your idea of being a good father?'

'What exactly are you talking about, Lauren?'

For once, standing on the stone steps, she was taller than him and could meet his eyes on the same level. 'The baby your wife is expecting — or have you detached yourself from it already?'

He shook his head, a smile beginning to curve his mouth. 'I haven't got a wife.'

It was Lauren's turn now to be perplexed. 'Kate?' she enquired dryly.

'Kate!' His laughter rippled round her. 'Kate is my sister-in-law! She's married to my brother, Daniel. They live in the States. Daniel's working there on a two-year exchange. He's a university lecturer — but also a dedicated Cornishman. That's why Kate came back here to have the baby. They want to make sure it's Cornish by birth.' Amusement deepened the blue of his eyes, hypnotising Lauren. 'I can't believe you really thought —'

'Thank you for sorting out the range,' she said curtly, taking Amy's hand and hurrying on up the steps, annoyance flooding through her. Yet again, she'd made herself look foolish by jumping to the wrong conclusion about this man. It was an easy mistake to make, she told herself as she stepped into the kitchen. But even so, she regretted making it.

Amy darted off to see the magic boat again, leaving her alone with Adam in front of the now-glowing range.

'That's the oven,' he said, pointing to one of the black iron doors. 'You probably have to judge its temperature by trial and error. Your great-aunt never seemed to have any problem, though if she did, she would never have admitted it. She wasn't that sort of person.'

'Did you see much of her?' Lauren enquired, taking the pasties out of their bag.

'There are some enamel plates you can put in the oven on that shelf, by your head,' Adam said. 'They'll probably need a wash, though. And the kettle's boiled; I left it ready.' He grinned. 'Until you can get the electric power switched back on, there's no instant hot water, I'm afraid.'

'But what about baths?'

'There's a copper in the outhouse. Next to the coal shed.'

'Copper?' Her horror couldn't be hidden.

'You fill it up with water, light a fire underneath, and when it's hot enough, use the tin bath that's hanging on the wall.'

'You're joking.'

He shook his head.

'I can't believe anyone could live like this.'

'Well, for many years your great-aunt did, until she had electricity put in.'

Lauren poured boiling water from the kettle into an enamelled bowl, reached out her hand to the tap, then looked enquiringly at him. 'Does cold water come out of this, or do I have to find a well?'

His eyes crinkled. 'I did fill the kettle from it.'

Cautiously, she turned the groaning tap, and a thin trickle descended into the sink. 'You haven't answered my question. How well did you know Aunt Hilda?'

'I used to come up here fairly frequently during her last years. She found things a bit difficult at times, though she'd never admit it.'

'She was in her nineties,' Lauren commented dryly, dipping a dusty dish into the hot water and rinsing it.

'I know, and you really would've liked her, Lauren. She was a fantastic lady. Wonderful artist, too. Extremely independent. And bright as a button, right to the end. That's how I learnt so much about you.'

Lauren tore a paper towel from the roll she'd bought earlier in Mrs Quin's shop, dried the dish, and placed the pasties on it. 'That's what I don't understand. She couldn't have known anything about me. I told you, I'd never met her, or even knew she existed until quite recently.'

'Well, she did,' he replied, opening the oven door for her. 'Mind! That's hot. Do you want me to find those photo albums for you?'

'I'll find them later, thank you, Mr Poldean,' Lauren said, washing lettuce under the tap. 'I should imagine it's time for your lunch anyway.'

'Is that an invitation?'

'No, it certainly isn't.' *How intrusive can he get?* she thought, fiercely slicing tomatoes.

'Then tomorrow you must come and eat with Kate and me. Sunday roast is one of my specialities. About half-past twelve?'

Without waiting for her answer, Adam swung his denim jacket over one shoulder and strode off down the hallway. Lauren heard his deep voice say goodbye to Amy as he passed the living room, then the front door slammed behind him.

As if he owns the place, she thought crossly.

4

There was a seat half-hidden amongst the lavender along one wall of the house, its wood bleached pale by years of salt winds and sunshine. Lauren sank down on it, resting her head against the warm stone behind her, closing her eyes, breathing in the sharp fragrance.

The drag of wave on shingle quivered the air. A blackbird flew down from the frond of an ancient tamarisk bush, one bright eye turned warily towards her, and dug its beak into the shaggy grass of the lawn.

Aunt Hilda left all this to me, Lauren thought, tension sliding away from her limbs. *But why?* It was a question that had puzzled her ever since she'd received the solicitor's letter:

Under the terms of the last will and testament of Hilda Laura Lelant, the property known as Seahaze in the village of Porthvose, Cornwall, with all its contents, is bequeathed to you ...

Hilda Laura Lelant. Laura, not quite Lauren though. Was there some significance? She let her thoughts rove back over the years, trying to glean what memories remained.

When contacted, the solicitor had explained that Great-aunt Hilda was her mother's aunt, her grandmother's sister. Unmarried. A maiden lady, as they termed it in those days. But had she always lived here, in Cornwall? Lauren wondered. And those photographs — Adam Poldean said she had albums full of them.

Adam Poldean. Blue eyes, laughing, from under a thick thatch of hair, wide mouth curving upwards into a smile ... So different from Duncan, with his immaculate, well-trimmed sleek head, and handsome chiselled features.

Lauren opened her eyes and shivered. The sun had vanished behind a dark cloud, turning the air chilly. Through a gap in the hedge the sea was grey and lumpy, flecked here and there with thin lines of whiteness that came and went. Seeing it, her mind flew to Amy, and fear flickered through her as she jumped up and hurried indoors, calling her daughter's name.

'I'm here, Mummy.' The little girl's voice came from the living room, and Lauren quickly joined her there. 'Look, the rainbow ship's stopped shining now. Has all the magic gone away?'

Lauren touched the silk of the child's hair. 'It'll sparkle again when the sun shines, sweetheart.'

'Tomorrow?'

'Maybe.'

Lauren's gaze searched the room. Somewhere in the house would be the albums. *Why didn't I let Adam show them to me when he was here earlier?* she thought with regret. There were so many other things she should be doing — cleaning the rooms from top to bottom for one — but finding those photographs suddenly had become far more important.

She looked at the glass-fronted bookcase. Volumes filled its shelves; old and well-read from the dilapidated state of their spines, she noticed. None appeared to be an album.

Her eyes turned to the drawers below, and she tugged at the tarnished brass handles of the top one. Letters, neatly tied into bundles by frayed ribbon, were stacked inside. She opened the second drawer, and the soft scent of lavender drifted up from the embroidered tablecloths and serviettes lying there.

Sitting back on her heels, Lauren surveyed the rest of the room. A cabinet of delicate china and glassware. A low round table. Two small cupboards set into corners on either side of the window, where Amy crouched on the window seat, looking mournfully at the glass galleon.

Faded chintz-covered armchairs and a drooping sofa surrounded the blackened brick fireplace, where tarnished brass bellows hung from a hook below the mantelpiece next to a three-pronged toasting fork. A huge wicker basket held a few logs, brass tongs and a poker. Ready for Aunt Hilda to appear any moment to tend the fire, Lauren thought. The whole room held an air of expectancy about it. As if waiting.

For what?

For whom?

She let her gaze rove on. There was such a clutter of bric-a-brac and ornaments. Every available surface was loaded with glass, silver and china. And then, in the darkest corner, partially hidden by an arm of the sofa, Lauren saw a stool heaped with brown leather-bound albums. Her excited intake of breath caught Amy's attention, and the child turned her head.

'Come and see,' Lauren said, picking up the topmost book and brushing away the film of dust with one hand.

Amy wrinkled her nose. 'It's old,' she complained, giving it a doubtful glance.

'And full of pictures,' Lauren explained, her fingers eagerly turning the thick, stiff pages where black and white photos clung, their corners held by triangles of sticky paper.

None of the faded ink-written names on the pages, or the faces, meant anything to Lauren as they looked at the people who had stared into the camera, self-consciously smiling, or frowning against the sun. Young men in bathing costumes that covered them like dark elongated vests from shoulder to thigh. Girls, wet hair tangled, in similar shapeless garments concealing their figures. All perched on rocks or posed in groups on sandy beaches bordered by cliffs.

'Boring, Mummy,' Amy protested. 'And I'm hungry. Is it dinner-time soon?'

Remembering the pasties, Lauren closed the album with a snap and rushed into the kitchen. A warm, savoury smell greeted her as she opened the oven door, and she couldn't resist a smile of pleasure, knowing that at last she had triumphed over the range. *Or Adam has*, an annoying little voice told her from somewhere inside her head.

'You promised we could go paddling this afternoon,' Amy said, biting into the crisp crust of pastry when they sat down at the table.

'But the sun's gone in now, sweetheart.'

'We can explore. There might be caves and mermaids and smugglers and pirates and treasure.'

'Not all at once,' Lauren laughed.

'There might,' her daughter insisted. 'I saw a mermaid this morning when I was on the beach talking to Adam.'

'Mr Poldean,' Lauren corrected her. 'It was probably a fish.'

'It *wasn't* a fish,' the little girl said firmly. 'It was a mermaid, and it had long floaty hair and a swishy silver tail.'

'Amy!'

'It did. I saw it.'

'Don't forget what happened to Pinocchio in the story,' Lauren warned.

'What happened?'

'His nose grew longer and longer when he told fibs.'

Amy tentatively rubbed a finger across the tip of her nose and frowned. 'Is mine growing longer?'

'Were you telling me fibs then?'

Carefully cutting a piece of cucumber

into small segments, Amy popped each one into her mouth before, ignoring Lauren's question, she replied, 'If we wear our anoraks, we won't be cold, will we?'

* * *

Later, as they descended the steps, Amy let out a shriek and began to race across the sand. 'It's Adam, Mummy.'

Lauren hesitated. He was there again, on the far side of the cove, sitting on some rocks and fishing. *My cove*, she thought. *His favourite place to fish*, she recalled Mrs Quin saying. *But not for long*, Lauren decided grimly, and began to walk purposefully across the beach.

'Range still going?'

A greeting destined to annoy, Lauren thought. 'Of course.'

'Did you stoke it up well before you came out?'

Her lips tightened. 'We're not going very far.'

She watched his dark brows flicker upwards, but was saved from his reply

48

as the line went taut, bending the end of the fishing rod, and he began to reel it in.

'Is it a fish?' Amy demanded, hopping up and down.

'Or a piece of seaweed?' Lauren suggested wryly.

The rod dipped more sharply. 'Can you fetch me that net?' He nodded to where it lay on the sand.

Lauren looked down and picked it up by the handle, then clambered onto the rock beside him.

'Dip it into the water. About there.' As she did so, he said, 'Deeper than that. It'll be a big fish. Can you see it?'

His weight leaned against her shoulder and she felt the catch of his cheek rough against hers, creating a pulse of excitement in her. There was no way she could move. The net was being tugged downwards by a sudden heaviness that made her sway.

Her feet were slipping on the wet granite. Any moment her legs would give way, and she would plummet into the waves that surged up around the rocks. Every muscle in her body ached with the effort of staying upright and keeping her grip on the handle of the net.

Adam's cold hands closed over hers, the line tossed aside, and she felt the net lift, their arms straining together as it came up through the water to reveal a mass of silvery brightness twisting and jerking in its depths.

'Is it a mermaid?' Amy breathed.

'I wish it was,' Adam chuckled, and the movement of his lips softly feathered Lauren's ear. 'My fortune would be made then, wouldn't it?'

Swiftly she turned her head away from such intimate contact, closing her eyes while he lifted the fish from the net and stunned it with one deft movement.

'Sorry about that,' he said, tipping the fish into a bucket. 'And it's not tomorrow's lunch, so you don't have to worry. I promised you a Sunday roast, and that's what it will be.'

He rose to his feet, swinging the bucket with one hand, the rod and net in the other, and stepped down from the rock to lay them on the shingle. Then, before Lauren could resist, his hands were firmly on either side of her waist, lifting her down.

For one long moment, her whole body rested against his, their faces level, her fingertips on his shoulders. She could see into the depths of his eyes, their clear blue darkened by rapidly widening pupils; the fringe of lashes surprisingly thick and long surrounding them. His mouth was only a fraction away from hers; his breath warming her skin.

Around her she could hear the rhythmic pound of wave on rock. Or was it the sound of her heartbeat throbbing in her ears? Time seemed to slow down, and her feet sank into the soft sand, her legs almost too weak to support her.

Adam's hands remained on her hips for a moment longer, steadying her, and then were gone. 'Until tomorrow,' he said softly, and was halfway across the cove before her own voice could echo, and then only in a whisper.

'Until tomorrow.'

5

After tea, Lauren played Snakes and Ladders, and Ludo, with Amy — games they'd discovered in one of the little wall cupboards by the living room window. To Amy they were completely new, and she revelled in their novelty, carefully shaking the dice and counting out the squares.

They skipped the little girl's usual bedtime bath. Lauren decided that heating the copper to fill the tin bath was a challenge for another day. Instead, she boiled the kettle for a quick cat's lick, as her own mother used to call it — flicking a flannel over face, neck and hands. The dried sand on Amy's legs and feet had already scattered itself around the house.

Surprisingly, the bookcase had revealed an ancient volume of nursery rhymes, complete with colour illustrations that were a delight just to look at, and fascinated Amy. There was also a copy of

Grimm's Fairy Tales, and Lauren made a mental note to sift through and choose only the less bloodthirsty ones, or at least edit out the gruesome bits when she read the stories aloud to her daughter.

Once she was upstairs and in her own bedroom overlooking the cove, it was only seconds before Amy was asleep, tired out by a day of sea and sunshine. Gazing down at the little girl's sun-flushed cheeks, Lauren decided to have an early night herself. She still had to find someone to check out the wiring and restore electric power to the house. Mrs Quin was probably the best person to ask; she was sure to know about everything in the village. But that would have to wait until tomorrow.

By half-past nine, Lauren was tucked up in the huge four-poster bed in what must have been Aunt Hilda's room, watching the last rays of the sun fade through a spectrum of red, pink and grey on the white walls.

Red sky at night, shepherd's delight, she mused. Tomorrow could well be another day of sunshine. Something to look forward to. And lunch with Adam and Kate.

★   ★   ★

I love you, love you, love you.

The voice sighed round her. Like velvet, Lauren thought drowsily. Warm. Caressing. A voice she didn't recognise.

Love you, love you ... The sound throbbed softly throughout the room, seeming to hang in the air, before fading into a whisper, like waves receding from the shore.

She lay there, heavy with sleep, a fierce excitement pulsing through her. Waiting, her eyes slowly growing used to the enveloping gloom until she could see the pale outline of the window. A full moon, hazed by a mist of salt covering the panes, appeared and slowly disappeared into a swirl of cloud.

Above her head, the canopy of the bed was lined with faded oyster-coloured silk. The hangings draped either side were

54

once deep blue, the colour still hidden in their folds. Each wooden post, ornately carved with flowers and leaves, rose up to be lost amongst them. Every item of furniture in the room was a dark shadow.

Love you, love you ...

It was a voice that she had heard, yet not heard. Familiar, yet unknown. But it created no fear, only a strange longing. Almost desire.

It was a while before she realised it had ceased, lost in the faint swish of waves sighing as they met the shore, way down in the cove.

The dream still clung to her. And Lauren was filled with a strange sense of regret.

★   ★   ★

'Is Aunt Hilda's house haunted?' she asked Adam the next day. She was carrying empty plates into the kitchen after they'd eaten thinly cut beef sliced from a huge joint, almost lost in an abundance of peas, freshly dug potatoes from the garden, broad beans, and tiny carrots. Adam's tanned forehead creased slightly at her question.

'Why, have you heard clanging chains and ghostly laughter?' Kate asked eagerly, delving into the fridge. 'Do you mind more strawberries, Lauren? We're overloaded with them.' She licked cream from her fingers as she took out a heaped bowl. 'It's probably smugglers entombed centuries ago in caves under the cliff, or spectral tinners still working down there in the mines. The ground's riddled with old workings round this way, you know.'

'Kate, do shut up!' Adam roared. 'You're scaring Lauren, and it's a good job Amy is out in the garden playing with the kittens.'

'What did make you ask, Lauren?' Kate said, ignoring him while she spooned the glowing fruit into glass dishes.

Lauren shrugged. 'Oh, nothing. I just wondered. Seeing as it's so old.'

'Oh, come on, Lauren,' Kate chuckled. 'Something must have triggered off the idea.'

'It really is nothing,' Lauren insisted.

She was aware of Adam's blue eyes studying her thoughtfully and could see he didn't believe her. *But if I told them about the voice,* she decided, *they'd think I was completely nutty.*

'Did you find those photographs?' Adam asked, tipping ground coffee into the percolator.

Lauren was grateful for the change of subject. 'Yes, but I haven't had a chance to look at them properly yet. The album I did flick through was of people on beaches.'

'Your great-aunt wasn't always reclusive, only when she became very old,' Adam said, steering her back into the dining room. 'Quite a social butterfly at one stage, I should imagine. She was very pretty in her youth. You're very much like her — especially without soot on your nose. How's that kitchen range?'

The colour in Lauren's cheeks deepened and her chin jutted. 'Burning brightly when we left,' she retorted, and sat down at the table again.

'Is this a special party?' Amy asked, coming in from the garden. 'Mummy made us put on our bestest clothes to come to see you.'

Lauren glanced down at the blue cotton skirt she was wearing. Somehow she hadn't been able to resist washing and brushing her shoulder-length hair until it gleamed like polished gold, and unpacking a crisp white sleeveless top to wear.

'It was just because my jeans were grubby from —'

'Battling with the kitchen range?' Adam enquired, with a teasing lift of one eyebrow.

'From washing down the kitchen walls and cleaning salt off the windows,' she retorted.

'OK. I'll believe you,' he replied.

'If everyone's finished eating, let's take our coffee into the garden, shall we?' Kate suggested.

'But first I'll wash up,' Lauren said. 'It's only fair, after you've provided such a fantastic meal.'

'And I'll dry,' Adam announced. When Lauren opened her mouth to protest, he added, 'You'll never find where we store all the dishes. And anyway, Kate should be putting her feet up for a while.'

The other woman had already gone out into the garden and settled herself on a sun-lounger under the shade of the trees. Amy lay on the grass beside her, playing with the kittens.

'It won't take long, and the coffee will be ready by the time we've finished,' Adam said, then added with a grin, 'You'll enjoy the luxury of using hot water from a tap.'

As he spoke, he unhooked a striped apron from the back of the door; and before Lauren could move away, his arms came round her waist while he tied its strings behind her. Even though it was merely a fleeting movement, his closeness disturbed her, and she stepped quickly sideways, turning on the tap with such force that the water splashed up and over her.

'You don't have to bathe in it, Lauren.'

'About the copper,' she said, seizing on a new subject with relief. 'Do I just fill it with water and light a fire underneath? That's what you said, isn't it?'

'I'll walk back with you this evening and show you.'

'No, thank you!' The words exploded from her.

Adam gave her a surprised look, then continued drying a glass dish.

Lauren took a deep breath. 'I have to learn how to do these things for myself,' she explained.

'But accepting some instruction can make it a lot easier for you,' he suggested, piling the dish on top of another on the table.

'I can work it out. I'm not stupid, you know.'

'I know you're not, Lauren, but we're living in the twentieth-first century now, whereas your great-aunt used those things for years before she had electricity laid on. It wasn't difficult for her.'

Lauren's back stiffened. 'I'm perfectly able to cope, thank you.'

He shrugged. 'Have it your own way, then. But don't forget, Lauren, I'm always here if you need help. Don't be afraid to ask, will you?'

★ ★ ★

'Will Amy be starting at the nursery school in the village?'

Tiptoeing cautiously past the sun-lounger to sit on the swinging seat, Lauren gave Kate a startled glance when she spoke.

'It's all right, you didn't wake me. I wasn't really asleep.' She laughed. 'Just had my eyes closed against the sun.'

Lauren frowned. 'I haven't really had time to think about it yet. Amy did go to a nursery school when we were staying with my friend Liz, after my divorce. She's got three-year-old twin boys, and so Amy went to one with them, just round the corner from where they live. She loved it.'

Moving the cushions to a more comfortable position behind her back, Lauren continued, 'She's really going to miss

Mark and Andy, so it'll be good for her to be with other children, I suppose.'

'Then what are you going to do up there in that old house on your own all day? Did you go to work before you came down here?'

'Sort of.'

Heaving herself into an upright position, Kate clasped one hand over her stomach and puffed out her cheeks. 'Will I be thankful when this little one arrives. I feel like a stranded whale. Hopefully it's not long now. If I get any bigger, I shall tip over flat on my face every time I stand up.' She picked up a straw hat from the grass beside her and began to fan her face. 'What do you mean by 'sort of'?'

'Well, after Amy was born, I worked from home illustrating books and designing cards and calendars. It wasn't very profitable, but I enjoyed it.'

'So you're an artist too, like your great-aunt. Most of the watercolours up there in the house were painted by her. I've got a beautiful one she gave me of the cove. It's on the wall in my bedroom. Remind me to show it to you when we go back indoors.'

Adam's voice came from behind them, and Lauren twisted her head to see him carrying a tray of coffee across the lawn.

'Cornwall is *the* place to come to paint,' he said, putting the tray on the grass and plumping down on the swing beside Lauren so that it swayed violently. 'Have you ever been to St Ives? The light there is fantastic, and there are lots of little galleries scattered round the town.'

Laughing, Lauren shook her head. 'I'm not that good.'

'Will you do a picture of me?' Kate asked. 'Just head and shoulders — not this mountain below. It's my husband Daniel's birthday at the end of next month, and that would make a fantastic present. Perhaps you could do one of the baby too, before we go back to the States?' Her round face shone with excitement. 'Or use it as a model for nativity Christmas cards. And Adam's kittens — they'd make wonderful paintings. People always go for animals, don't they? When could you start? You'll have half the day free, with Amy at nursery school.'

'Kate!' Adam warned. 'You're doing it again.'

'Doing what?'

'Organising other people's lives. Perhaps Lauren has her own ideas for how to fill her day. Though by the time she's boiled water in the copper and kept that kitchen range going, I don't imagine there'll be much left over for artistic activity — not even a charcoal drawing,' he teased.

'You'll want to have the house modernised a bit though, won't you, Lauren?' Kate said. 'All it needs, once the electricity is put back on, is a cooker, washing machine, tumble drier — oh and a fridge, and ... '

'Kate!' Adam laughed.

'Sorry!'

'Drink your coffee,' he suggested, then turned to Lauren. 'What are your plans for the place, or is it too early to think about that yet?'

Lauren sighed, remembering her desperate rush to get away before Duncan and Naomi could start putting on the pressure about taking Amy. 'I didn't even know about Aunt Hilda, or that she'd left me her house, until a couple of months ago. It was a complete surprise. After my ... divorce ... ' The word caught in her throat. 'My husband, Duncan — ex-husband,' she quickly corrected herself. 'Duncan sold our own and I received half its value. Not a great deal, though. There was a big mortgage to pay off, and by the time that was sorted out... ' Her mouth drooped. 'That money is all I have for Amy and me to live on. It was silly of me, but I refused to accept maintenance from Duncan. It had to be a complete break. Only, now ... ' She breathed in deeply and swallowed the lump rising into her throat. 'He and Naomi, his new wife, and her children are going to live in New Zealand. Duncan's been offered a job with a law firm out there. And he wants to take Amy with them.'

'But you're her mother, Lauren. They

can't do that, can they?' Kate protested, spooning sugar into her coffee and slowly stirring it.

'I really don't know, Kate. I didn't stay long enough to find out. Duncan's a solicitor, so can probably work out a way. When I received his letter the other morning, telling me what he intends to do, I panicked, packed a few things, and drove straight down here.' Pausing, she breathed in deeply, trying to steady her voice before continuing. 'We'd been staying with Liz, an old school friend of mine, and her family since the house was sold.' She brushed one hand across her cheek. 'Here was the only place I could think of to escape to. You see, Duncan doesn't know about Aunt Hilda leaving her property to me.'

'So it must have been a terrible shock to discover what a dilapidated state it's in, then, Lauren,' Adam mused, leaning forward to pour coffee into their cups. 'Electricity cut off. Dust and damp everywhere. And the whole place in a time warp.'

Lauren shuddered, remembering the feeling of despair that had overwhelmed her when she'd unlocked the front door and stumbled inside, to discover herself in total darkness, with only the car torch to find their way around.

'Oh, you poor darling!' Kate burst out impetuously. 'You must stay here with us, mustn't she, Adam?'

'No, I couldn't do that. We'll be fine.' She took the cup that Adam handed to her, trying to steady it as the swing moved, very aware of the closeness of his body beside her.

'Ted Quin would check out all the electrical bits and renew anything that's not up to much, wouldn't he, Adam?' Kate was already rushing on, making plans. 'Lauren and I can go round the sale rooms and second-hand shops in Penzance to find everything she needs.'

Adam rested his head against the back of the swinging seat and explained to Lauren, 'Ted was an electrician before he retired, and still does odd jobs now and then. But whether he could take on something like that ...'

'Oh, don't be such a pessimist, Adam!' Kate remonstrated. 'Of course he'll do it. Mrs Quin's always complaining about him having nothing to keep him occupied apart from his garden. I'm sure if you have a word with him ... You know, he thinks the world of you since you sorted out his tax return and he got that refund. If not, we'll have to win over Mrs Quin. Ted does exactly what she tells him.'

'He doesn't have a great deal of choice!'

Kate gave Lauren a contented smile. 'There. All sorted. You've got a car, haven't you, so we can pop over to Penzance after you've taken Amy to the nursery in the morning. You see, it's part of Adam's school. Sort of joined on. Right next to the church.'

Bemused by Kate's rapid chatter, Lauren could only nod in agreement.

'So there you are, Lauren.' Adam said, his mouth curving into a smile. 'With Kate in control, every minute of your life will be completely organised from now on.' He glanced across to where Amy was sitting under a tree, with kittens squirming over her lap. 'Why don't you bring Amy along tomorrow? See how she likes it. And you really don't need to worry — I'll be there to keep an eye on her, I promise.'

6

Lauren was relieved to find that when she tried to start her car the following morning, the dampness had dried out in the sunshine, and the engine fired first time.

'I was right, wasn't' I?' Kate said as they drove along the road towards Penzance. 'Amy couldn't wait to join the other children, could she?'

'So what does that say about me?' Lauren asked regretfully, stifling a yawn. 'Sorry, but I've been up since five. Amy came in to wake me, all dressed and ready for nursery school.' She gave a rueful smile. 'T-shirt inside out with the label at the front, a pair of old blue denim jeans pulled up to her armpits, and her trainers on the wrong feet.'

'Adam has that effect on females!' Kate chuckled. 'They can't wait to be with him.' She pointed through the car window. 'Look! There's St Michael's Mount. Over that hedge — see it?'

Lauren followed the direction to where the outline of an island appeared hazily through early-morning mist. Grey walls, seemingly part of the granite rock, rose from the top.

'Not sure I can make it right up to the castle in my present elephantine state,' Kate said ruefully, wrinkling up her nose. 'It's a steep climb when you get over there. You need the tide out to cross the causeway, too — though there are little boats, so maybe we could do that. But Adam's quite an authority on the history of the castle. He'll take you up there some time.'

Traffic was beginning to build up as they approached the town. 'There's a car park at the top of the hill,' Kate said. 'Save us walking. I doubt I should ever make it. And there's a brilliant place for coffee and homemade cakes almost opposite. We'll go there.'

Kate knew every inch of the town. 'I was born in Newlyn,' she explained, biting into a fat chocolate éclair after they'd toured the shops for nearly an hour. 'Now, let's see. The cooker, fridge, and washing machine will be delivered tomorrow afternoon ...' She frowned. 'I really don't understand why that wretched man couldn't make it today. But at least we've got the microwave, even though you can't use it until the electricity is sorted out.'

'It would've been next week if you hadn't forced his hand,' Lauren said with a smile. 'Marching to the door like you did, saying we'd find another more helpful shop — I'd never have dared do that.'

'He was just being difficult. An order's an order, especially in this day and age. If he wants your money, then he should be prepared to deliver immediately. After all, everything was in the shop, right there in front of us. He was just being ... ' She stopped and grinned at Lauren. 'Awkward. It really annoys me that you have to be so pushy to get anything done.'

'Well, I'd never have been able to do that.'

'Then it's a good job you had me with you! Oh, this éclair is gorgeous. Why on earth didn't you have one? You can eat a Danish pastry anywhere, but these are a speciality here.' She gave her stomach a pat and chuckled. 'I bet little thumper is going to enjoy it. They do a fantastic steak pie at lunchtime — pastry like a wisp of heaven.' Wiping a scrap of cream from around her mouth with a paper serviette while she continued talking, her words were muffled. 'It's a shame Ted Quin couldn't come this afternoon to sort out what needs to be done, but it's his day to go over to the Cash and Carry for Mrs Quin, and I suppose the shop does have to take precedence. Anyway, you'll have to stay in tomorrow for the cooker and things to arrive, so Ted will be able to make sure they're properly connected up, once he's checked out the wiring or whatever needs doing. I'll bring you up some more strawberries when the fridge is installed and you can store cream. Have you finished that coffee?'

Having a job to keep up with Kate's

butterfly brain as it flitted from subject to subject, Lauren gulped down the last dregs and nodded.

'OK then, we've got time to go down to Marazion on the way home. You'll have a better view of St Michael's Mount from there. If we're lucky, the tide will be out and we can walk across the causeway.'

'But no climbing up to the castle,' Lauren warned. 'Delivering babies isn't one of my specialities.'

'You do worry, don't you, Lauren?' Kate said, easing herself away from the edge of the table. 'Besides, little Thumper's not due for days yet.'

Even so, Lauren couldn't help being anxious later, as they crossed the flat wet stones of the causeway. Kate only had to slip …

'Oh, really, Lauren. Don't fuss! You're as bad as Adam.'

Tiny wavelets rippled the edges of the strip of sand on either side, retreating to leave shallow pools, with trails of yellow-brown seaweed festooning the rocks. Ahead, Lauren could see a horseshoe-shaped little harbour where small boats lolled on their sides, waiting for the next tide to flood back in and refloat them.

Behind her, the houses of Marazion, tinted in shades of cream, white and pink, intermingled with those of harsh grey granite, stretching away from a sloping sandy beach. Sunshine glinted on windows, turning them into flashing beacons.

Overhead a helicopter circled low, the drone of its engine clattering down through the still air, before it headed away towards the Scillies with its load of holidaymakers.

They were climbing the cobbled slope beside the harbour wall, when Kate suddenly clasped one hand to her side and gasped.

'Are you all right?'

'It's only a stitch. Do stop clucking, Lauren. You're like a mother hen.'

The words were curt. *Unusual for Kate*, Lauren thought. *But perhaps she's like that. Changeable. After all, I hardly know her.*

Kate led the way to a wooden seat opposite a small shop that sold postcards and souvenirs, her round face rosy as she sank down in the shade.

'Do you want to come in, or wait out here while I buy a card?' Lauren asked, deciding she must let her friend Liz know she was OK. She and Amy had left in such a panic and rush, and Liz would be worrying.

'Stay here. Looks a bit of a squash in there,' Kate replied.

'I'll only be a couple of minutes then.'

By the time she'd chosen a suitable view of St Michael's Mount, then queued to pay behind a group of foreign students who were having a problem with the correct money, it took far longer than that. But when she came out again, Kate hadn't moved and was sitting, eyes closed.

'Are you sure you're feeling all right?'

'The sun's a bit bright, that's all,' Kate replied, and stood up, rubbing the small of her back as she did so. 'Let's go into the café and have something to eat, shall we?'

'You can't be hungry again, Kate! Not after that huge chocolate éclair.'

'I am eating for two, don't forget.'

'Well, we mustn't be too long, Kate. Amy will be out of nursery school in an hour, and I need to be there to collect her,' Lauren reminded her. 'I'll just write this card. There's a post-box over by the wall.'

They were drinking more coffee and eating crusty rolls filled with home-cooked ham, when Lauren casually asked, 'Has Adam ever been married?'

Kate brushed a crumb from her chin and shook her head. 'Years back he was engaged, though. Someone he met at university, I think.' Taking another bite of the roll, she chewed it thoughtfully. 'It was well before I started going out with Daniel, so I never knew her, but … ' Glancing at her watch, her eyes widened. 'Whoops, it's getting late. We'd better go down to the causeway before the tide comes back in. You mustn't be late for Amy.' Tossing the crumbs left on her plate to where a grey-backed gull strutted along the top of the wall, slowly she stood up, one hand pressed against her back.

To Lauren's dismay, the tide was well in, and the causeway completely covered by the time they reached it.

'Don't look so worried,' Kate said, reading her expression. 'I told you there are ferries to take people across to Marazion. Come on, we'll catch one of those.'

Reaching the stone jetty of the harbour, they joined a small queue of people climbing one by one into a swaying little boat. Once it was filled, they had to wait for another to arrive from Marazion. Clinging tightly to Lauren's arm, Kate went sideways down to the bottom of the wet steps, where a bronzed ferryman steadied her while she lowered herself over the side.

'Mebbe we'd best let you have this one to yourself, m'dear,' he suggested, winking one eye at her.

But for once Kate was silent, her knuckles white as they gripped the edge of the narrow seat, and again Lauren gave her an anxious glance. When they

78

were back in the car, she began to relax, becoming her chatterbox self again.

'Well, that wasn't so terrifying, was it, Lauren?' she asked. 'Now you've experienced both ways of reaching the island, which do you prefer?'

'Oh, the causeway every time. When you mentioned a ferry, I thought it was something far larger, not a tiny little craft like that one. And then, landing by that huge rock …'

'That's the only way back to the beach when the tide is in. It would look awful if they erected a landing stage on such a beautiful stretch of sand. Spoil it completely. Now, when we reach Porthvose, you can show me around your great-aunt's house. I'm dying to see it. It sounds so primitive. Do you really have to bathe in a tin tub, and boil water in a copper? Adam said you were having terrible trouble trying to light the range when he called the other day. Covered from head to toe in smuts like a little chimney sweep, was how he described you.'

Her eyes swivelled round. 'Is your hair really that gorgeous colour, or do you colour it? Mine's such a mess.' Pulling at a strand, she went cross-eyed trying to look at it. 'All thin and wispy. I suppose it's a result of little Thumper.' She sighed. 'Oh, I shall be glad when it's all over and I'm back to looking human again.'

'You look fantastic,' Lauren said, trying hard to follow the ever-changing thread of Kate's conversation as she steered the car past Mrs Quin's shop. 'And, yes, we do.'

'Do what?'

'Bathe in a tin tub.'

'How awful!'

They were outside the house now, and Lauren helped Kate ease her heavy body up from the car seat, and guided her along the path.

'Oh, what a wonderful view you have from here. You can watch the sea from every window. And all that lavender, too. It'll smell wonderful when it's in full bloom. And think of all the lavender bags you can make. Why don't you set up a craft stall somewhere? Sell your paintings and the cards you design. The grockles would love it.'

'Grockles?'

'Tourists! It's what we call them. Oh, this really is a beautiful house. All those beams. And the furniture. It must be worth a fortune. Is that the way to the beach? Can I go down there? Through here? This must be the range Adam told me about. It really does look a pig, like he said. How on earth do you manage to cook?'

'Well, thanks to you and yesterday's Sunday lunch, I haven't really had to do any proper cooking yet,' Lauren said, squeezing in a word while Kate paused for breath to open the back door. 'Look, I really must go and collect Amy. She'll be frantic if I'm not there.'

'Adam will be keeping an eye on her. He's fantastic with the children. Been at that school ever since he qualified, and now he's head teacher. Don't worry, she'll be fine. Does the tide come right up to this mark?'

'Where?' Lauren peered down at the

stone steps Kate was already descending.

'Here. This line of seaweed. See? It's probably only when there's a really bad storm. You are so lucky, living in a place like this. Adam must envy you. He's always wanted to live up here. Really loves the place. He was hoping to buy it after Miss Trevaunance died.'

Lauren paused on the top step. *Does that explain why Adam keeps returning to the house?* she mused. *Because he loves it so much?*

'I really have to go and fetch Amy now, Kate. Why don't you stay in the garden until we get back? It's lovely and cool on the seat over there, amongst the lavender.'

Climbing back up the steps, Kate said, 'Sure you don't want me to come with you?'

'No, I'd rather do it on my own.'

All Lauren wanted was to have Amy back with her again, and to listen to how her day had gone.

Maybe, too, she would see Adam.

Amy was sitting on top of the grey stone wall outside the school, deep in conversation with Adam, when Lauren drove up, breathless. 'I'm so sorry to be late,' she gasped. 'Kate and I....'

Adam laughed. 'Enough said, Lauren. You're lucky to have escaped at all. I bet she's worn you out with all her chatter.'

Lauren smiled. 'Well, we have crammed quite a lot into the morning. I thought she looked a bit tired, so I've left her sitting in my garden. Thanks for keeping an eye on Amy.' She bent to kiss the little girl. 'How's it been?'

'I've made lots and lots of friends. There's a girl called Morwenna. That's a funny name, isn't it, Mummy? And another called ...' She frowned, trying to remember. 'I think it was Demerara, like that brown sugar we make the cakes with.'

'Demelza,' Adam prompted. 'Both good old Cornish names. Now,' he said, lifting her down from the wall, 'you'd best be going home with your mummy and have some lunch.' Recalling the ham rolls she and Kate had eaten earlier, Lauren felt rather guilty.

Back at the house, she looked out of the window as she filled the kettle, but there was no sign of Kate on the seat outside. Leaving Amy with a cheese sandwich and mug of apple juice, she went out into the garden. Kate, she saw, was on the beach, paddling along the water's edge, her trainers carried in one hand, her skirt gathered into the other.

'Hi, Lauren! Come and join me. It's glorious down here.'

'You're mad, Kate!' Lauren said, running down the steps and across the warm sand.

Bending to peer into the swirls of sandy water, Kate pointed. 'Look! A tiny crab. Can you see it? There! Oh!' Her face suddenly contorted.

'What's up? Has it bitten you?' Lauren teased, and then her laughter died. 'What's wrong, Kate? Is it the baby?'

She nodded slowly, her eyes wide with pain, her breath held tight. A wave swept in, roaring across the beach, soaking Lauren's sandals. The sun had vanished now, hidden in a growing bank of cloud, leaving the air chill and damp. Goose-pimples prickled her skin.

'The baby's not due for days yet,' Kate whispered, her cold fingers reaching out to catch hold of Lauren's hand. 'It can't be happening now. It shouldn't hurt like this, should it? Did it when you had Amy? Oh, Lauren, I'm so frightened.'

'No need to be,' Lauren said, hoping her voice sounded reassuring. 'Babies often come early. And don't worry — there's nothing to it. Women are having babies all the time.'

But not here, she told herself. *Not in the middle of an empty beach with the tide rushing in.* 'Can you make it back to the house?'

Teeth biting into her white lips, Kate nodded, her feet moving forward mechanically, step by step. Supporting her with one arm, Lauren gently urged her on, while her own mind spun.

Without electricity, she hadn't been

able to recharge her mobile phone. *How am I going to get help?* she wondered. *I can't leave Kate while I run down to the village. And what about Amy? If the baby comes while I'm gone ...*

But babies don't arrive that quickly, do they, she reasoned. *It can take hours. Days even. How long did Amy take? Nearly twelve hours.*

Kate's fingers gripped more tightly, the nails scoring deep into Lauren's palm, and she heard the accompanying intake of breath. This baby wasn't going to wait.

'Almost there,' she comforted, helping Kate up the first step. 'Only five more ... four ... three ... two ... That's it. You're doing brilliantly. It's not far along the path now. OK? Let me undo the door.'

She could see Amy curled up on the window seat, deeply engrossed in watching the glass galleon, as they passed the room and began to climb the stairs, pausing frequently while another spasm enveloped the terrified woman.

'Don't leave me, will you, Lauren? Please don't leave me.'

'Only for a minute, Kate. I promise. Lie down on the bed while I go and find some of the linen and towels we bought this morning. I'll be right back. That's it. Just lie down there.'

She caught a glimpse of her own tense face in the dressing-table mirror as she unwrapped the packages. *What am I going to do?* she asked herself, her heart thudding as she gathered them up. *What am I going to do?* Panic was rising inside her, stiffening her limbs so that she could hardly make her feet move across the room.

'Lauren!' The desperate cry frightened her. 'Oh, Lauren, I never thought it would be like this,' Kate sobbed.

Lauren caught the trembling hands and held them tight. 'Everything is going to be all right, Kate,' she soothed. 'There's nothing to worry about at all.'

And, desperately, wished she could believe that herself.

7

'Just relax, Kate. Everything's going to be fine. You've been to prenatal classes while you've been staying here, haven't you?'

Kate nodded weakly, her mouth quivering.

'And practised deep breathing?'

Another slight nod.

'Right then, let's try it, shall we? Ready?' Lauren glanced down at the little gold watch on her wrist as the next pain ended, mentally counting. Her own body was relaxing a little as she began to breathe in rhythm with the other woman, giving her encouragement.

There was a rustle of movement by the door and Amy appeared, her small face anxious. 'Why's Kate crying like that, Mummy?'

'Her baby's being born, sweetheart. Now, I want you to go back downstairs and find those lovely old books of Aunt Hilda's, then you can sit on the window seat and look at them. Will you do that for me, Amy?'

The child turned slowly, and Lauren heard her feet patter down the stairs. But seconds later she was back again, with the glass galleon carefully held in her hands.

'Sweetheart, I said ... ' Lauren began, but Amy interrupted her by tiptoeing across the room to place the galleon on the bed.

'It's magic, Kate,' she explained solemnly. 'You just make a wish, and it will come true. Would you like to borrow it until your baby is born?'

Through her tears, Kate smiled and nodded. As she did so, a shaft of sunshine slipped through the diamond panes of the window to touch one of the tiny sails, and a fiery glow began to radiate forth into rainbows of colour.

Amy's face was transfixed, her eyes wide with excitement. 'Quick, Kate, make a wish.'

Kate's gaze was on the shimmering

brightness, and her lips curved into silent movement.

'I'll come back and fetch it when your baby's born, then I can say hello,' Amy assured her, and with a last lingering glance at the galleon, she went out through the door.

'She's made her own wish,' Lauren told Kate. 'And I know she'll be devastated if it doesn't come true.'

'Has she told you what it is?'

Lauren was relieved to hear that Kate's voice had lost its panic-stricken note.

Someone to want us again.

'It breaks the spell if you tell a wish,' she said.

As Lauren put the glass galleon on the chest of drawers beside the bed, where it glinted in the sunshine, Kate asked, 'Do you think its magic will work for me?'

Giving Kate's cold hand a squeeze, Lauren smiled back at her. 'I'm sure it will.' And then, with her gaze fixed on the tiny galleon, she made her own silent wish: *Please, oh please send someone to help us.*

Almost at the same moment, a sharp rat-a-tat on the front door made her spin round. She ran down the stairs to open it.

'Adam!' she whispered. 'Thank goodness you're here.'

'Amy left her anorak behind,' he said, holding it out to her. Then his expression changed. 'What's wrong, Lauren? You look like death.'

'It's Kate. The baby's on its way. She's upstairs.'

Before she could say any more, he was across the hall and taking the stairs two at a time. Lauren followed more slowly, her breath sighing out with relief. Adam was here. Now everything would be all right.

Kate's head was buried into his shoulder when Lauren entered the room.

'Probably just a false alarm,' he comforted. 'Too many strawberries, I expect.'

Kate's head shot up and she glowered across at Lauren. 'Men!' she gritted through clenched teeth. 'Typical! I do know the difference between a stomach ache and this, Adam.'

'It's getting urgent, Adam. The pains

are very close now,' Lauren murmured quietly into his ear.

'Enough time to drive her to the hospital?'

She shook her head. 'No way!'

He tugged his mobile phone from a pocket and keyed in a number. 'Damn! There's no signal up here. I'll have to go closer to the village.'

Amy's footsteps were coming up the stairs, but Adam was already opening the door.

'Ah,' he said. 'Just the young lady I was looking for. Do you remember the wall by the big window in your classroom, Amy? With all the pictures that the boys and girls have drawn?'

'Course I do.'

'Will you make a very special one for me to put up there? You'll find a box of felt-tip pens and a pad of paper in my bag. I left it on the chair by your front door. And the kitchen table is nice and wide, so that's the best place for drawing.'

'What sort of drawing?'

'How about the kittens? You could

make a separate picture for each of them, but do it very slowly and carefully, and I'll be back soon to see what you've done.'

How can he be so calm and practical at a time like this? Lauren marvelled, amazed at the way Adam had distracted her daughter so easily. Then the front door closed and she heard the sound of his feet running down the lane.

* * *

The baby was a boy. 'And a true little Cornishman,' Kate murmured, one finger stroking the soft dark down of his head.

The paramedics had arrived in an ambulance, too late for the birth to take place at the hospital. 'Head is already there,' one of them had announced. 'You'll want to stay with Katherine, won't you, sir? Hold her hand?'

'I'm not the father,' Adam protested, his face registering acute horror.

'I will,' Lauren said, moving to the side of the four-poster.

'Always nice to have a friendly face

there. Now, come on Katherine. One more big push. Ready?'

Feeling perfectly calm now that some- one else had taken over, Lauren gently clasped Kate's hand, trying not to cry out herself as the fingers closed into a vice-like grip. And suddenly, there was this fragile little scrap of humanity lying, towel-wrapped, in Kate's arms.

The miracle of birth, she thought. Something she'd experienced herself, but never witnessed so closely with someone else before.

There was a knock on the bedroom door, and Adam stood there, carrying a tray of mugs. 'Isn't tea what's called for at this stage?' he enquired, a twinkle of humour in his blue eyes. 'Amy and I heard the baby cry — and I'm having a terrible job to hold her back any longer. Could she just have a peep?'

The little girl's face, when she gazed down at the baby, was a picture of delight and awe. 'Almost as small as a kitten,' she breathed, leaning against the side of the bed and smiling up at Kate. 'Have you got wobbly bits on your tummy to feed it milk, like mummy cats do?'

* * *

Later, Adam and Lauren sat together, drinking more tea. Amy had finally been put to bed, still asking questions that Adam answered, quietly and simply.

'When a child requests knowledge, it has to be the truth,' he told Lauren. 'At this age, it's far easier for them to accept what later can become distorted by others. And if you always tell her the truth, Amy won't be afraid to ask when things trouble her, and she'll trust you.'

Sipping her tea, Lauren looked at him through her lashes. He almost filled one of the chintz-covered armchairs, his head resting against the back of it, his long denim-clad legs stretched out, completely relaxed. *Just as if it's his home and he belongs here*, she thought. *And maybe he does. After all, he's been in this house far more often than I have. He knows every inch of it, and where everything is kept.*

I'm the stranger. The outsider.

'Do you feel lonely up here, right on the edge of the sea, Lauren?'

She lowered her eyes from his penetrating gaze. 'Not really. Just a bit ... well, strange, I suppose. A new home always takes a while to get used to. And now, with Amy at nursery school ... ' Her voice trailed away. *I'm being pathetic, she decided. It's been a long day. And with all that's happened ... I'm just tired.*

'I'll soon get used to being here,' she continued. 'It's our home now. Mine and Amy's.' She said the last words forcefully, remembering this was the house Adam wanted for his own. And no way was she going to part with it.

'What happens if your ex-husband finds where you're living?'

Lauren's chin jutted. 'He won't.'

'Can you be sure of that?'

'Only my friend Liz knows where we are, and there's no way she'll tell him. He doesn't even know I have this house. He'll never find us here.'

Getting up from the chair, Adam put

his mug back onto the table. 'Well, I hope you're right. Now I'm off to visit Kate in the hospital. See you in the morning, Lauren.'

For a moment, he paused, looking down at her with an expression she couldn't read, before he stepped into the hall, opened the front door and was gone.

The room seemed empty, as if there was a void; the cushion of the chair still dented from where he'd been sitting. Lauren reached out a hand and touched it, feeling the warmth of him remaining there. Then she gathered up their mugs and went into the kitchen to boil the kettle and wash them.

As her hands delved into the bowl, Adam's words echoed in her head: *What happens if your ex-husband finds out where you're living?* And her own reply: *'He won't.'*

How could he? Only Liz knew where she was living now, and Lauren knew she would never tell Duncan. Liz hated him. It was the one thing that had marred their friendship.

She recalled how, on the day of Duncan's wedding to Naomi, Liz had found her weeping.

'You can't go on breaking your heart forever, Lauren. Duncan isn't worth it. He wasn't right for you. All your friends told you that, didn't they?'

'I love him, Liz.'

'Are you certain of that, Lauren? Isn't it just that you were swept off your feet by such a good-looking man? Duncan's a charmer. Always has been. Always will be. Women will constantly fall under his spell. He enjoys that. It flatters his ego. And he will never be faithful to anyone.'

'You can't say that, Liz —'

'I'm not dazzled by him, like you. He was never the right man for you, Lauren. One day, when you do meet the right one, you'll realise that. And you *will* meet him.' Her eyes had a faraway look as she continued, 'Every person in the world has a complementary half waiting somewhere. It's merely a matter of finding them, that's all.'

'Not every marriage is like yours, Liz.'

'It is if you marry the right person.'

* ★ *

'I had such a strange dream when I was lying in your beautiful four-poster bed yesterday,' Kate said, when Lauren went to collect her and the baby from the hospital the following morning, and they were driving back through the village. 'It was as though there was a voice whispering softly.' Then, meeting Lauren's startled gaze, she continued thoughtfully, 'Maybe it wasn't a dream, though. On Sunday you asked whether your great-aunt's house was haunted. Is that the reason?'

Easing the car into another gear, Lauren smiled back at her. 'Of course you were dreaming, Kate. And no wonder, after all that had happened to you.' She hoped her words were convincing as she reflected that last night was the first time she hadn't heard the voice. Was it because she'd slept in Amy's room because she hadn't made up her own bed again, too tired after clearing it of all the sheets and towels from earlier? Did that mean the voice was connected with Great-aunt Hilda's bedroom — and the four-poster?

There was such a depth of feeling to it when she heard it. Such longing. Could intense emotion be captured and held, suspended in time? If so, whose voice was it? And to whom was it speaking?

Her mind recalled the bureau with its drawer filled with bundles of letters. Would they give the answer?

'Just think,' Kate was saying, her voice already racing on. 'It won't be long before we're back in the States. I can't wait for us all to be together again. It's been such an age since I saw Daniel. I know there's Skype and all that on the internet, but it's not the same as being together.'

'Leaving so soon?' Lauren's voice was filled with sadness at the thought of losing this new friend.

'It's been over a month. Could you bear to be away from the one you love for over a month? Oh, Lauren, I'm so sorry. I didn't think … '

'Have you decided on a name yet?'

Lauren interrupted swiftly.

'We thought we'd wait until we saw what the baby looked like first. After all, you couldn't call him Rufus if he has a thatch of black hair, can you? Or Goliath, if he turns out to be a puny little scrap.'

'You must have some idea.'

Kate grinned. 'Abigail or Sarah. You see, I was convinced it would be a girl. But whatever we choose, his middle name will be Adam. It couldn't be anything else, could it?'

★　★　★

There was a celebration lunch on the Sunday before Kate and the baby left for America. Somehow, Lauren felt, it wasn't the same as the previous time. For one thing, it rained. Rain, she noticed, was different in Cornwall. It wasn't like the rain she'd known at home. This was a soft, misty drizzle that hung in the air, clinging to eyelashes and hair like gossamer.

With Amy huddled beside her under the umbrella, she walked down the hill to

Adam's thatched cottage, the cliffs hidden so thoroughly by a thin mist, it was as if they didn't exist. Only the whispering sea gave any hint in which direction the beach lay, and even that was muted.

She could imagine this cove as it had been once, centuries ago. A haunt of wreckers and smugglers. And on a day such as this, those jagged rocks must have captured many a rich bounty to bring tinners and fisherfolk leaping down to the sandy shore. Who had lived in Great-aunt Hilda's house then? she wondered. It was in an ideal position for storing smuggled booty.

The wet wood of Adam's gate slid under her fingers as she pushed it, a spatter of raindrops brushing her face from the drooping branches of a tree. She remembered the first time she'd walked up this path. The smell of coffee. The welcome. And suddenly her life felt empty.

Goodbyes are never happy. Even though they'd only known each other for so few days, Lauren regarded Kate as a close friend, and was going to miss her — and the baby. When Lauren returned to the house that evening, she was verging on tears. The days ahead seemed bleak and lonely without Kate's constant chatter.

Lavender trailed against her legs as she brushed past the bushes and recollected Kate's parting words. 'You won't forget my idea about a craft shop, will you, Lauren?'

Adam had echoed her words. 'Craft shop?'

'To sell Lauren's paintings and cards,' Kate explained. 'Don't you think it's a great idea?'

'Maybe we could go over to St Ives sometime,' he suggested. 'That's the place for art galleries and quaint little shops.'

But even the idea of a day spent with Adam didn't cheer Lauren.

It was later that evening that she picked up the photograph albums and began to turn the pages, seeing pictures of herself from babyhood carefully pasted there. But why? Why should Great-aunt Hilda even care? *And why did my mother send them to her?* Lauren asked herself. For it could only have been her mother. No one else would.

Her gaze turned to the bureau standing against the far wall, and she remembered the drawer. It was only a small one. Kneeling down, she tugged it out. Bundles of letters lay inside, neatly banded with narrow ribbon, faded to a shade of nothingness. Lauren looked at them. *These belonged to my great-aunt. Letters to be read only by her. If anyone else were to do so, it would be an intrusion into her life. But how else am I to know her?* she thought. *This distant figure who kept such a permanent record of me.*

She wanted to close the drawer. Shut out the past. But the temptation was too strong. She had to know. Had to understand the old lady who'd lived in solitude, retaining her hold on the years that had gone before, never changing. As if time had stood still, Lauren thought. Maybe, for her, it had.

Gathering the bundles together, Lauren

carried them upstairs to the four-poster bed, to read before she slept that night.

8

It was gone three o'clock before Lauren turned off the light; and when she did, she was lost in a world of romance. If only someone could write letters like that today, she wished. Each sentence was a poem of infinite beauty.

They were all in date order. The first was written in 1942. A polite and formal letter. Aunt Hilda would have been a teenager then, except no one called them that in those days, Lauren reasoned. The address at the top of the letter was a nearby stately home, and she guessed it had been requisitioned as a military hospital. So many were during the war, for those recovering from their wounds.

The local church had organised a tea party for the patients there. Hilda was helping. One man had written to thank her for her kindness to him that day, making him forget he was, and always would be, a cripple. It was signed *Matthew Poldean*. The surname startled Lauren, until she realised it was quite a common Cornish one in this part of the country.

From then onwards, Hilda and Matthew communicated regularly, the tone of his letters changing as the months passed, growing more passionate. Reading them, Lauren wondered what her great-aunt's replies had been to warrant such devotion. Had she written back in the same adoring terms?

After Matthew was discharged from the navy on account of his injuries, and returned to his family home in Sennen Cove, a few miles away near Land's End, they met more frequently, and wrote nearly every day. Those meetings, Lauren could tell, sparked an even greater fire in him.

I love you, love you, love you, his letters ended only weeks later, when they became secretly engaged.

Lauren read on avidly, all qualms forgotten, eager to discover what happened. But suddenly the letters ceased, and the final one in the bundle gave no hint of the reason why.

I love you, love you, love you, my beloved one. Until we meet again, your ever adoring, Matthew.

That was how that letter had ended. It puzzled her. Maybe they'd had a quarrel. But two so much in love would reunite. They couldn't have kept apart. So why?

Would Adam know? He'd visited Aunt Hilda frequently in her last years. Did she confide in him? Adam was the kind of man people did confide in.

Lauren's eyes were heavy with sleep. *Tomorrow*, she decided, yawning, *I'll ask him.*

*   *   *

I love you, love you, love you. When Lauren heard the voice quivering the air, this time she knew what to do.

'Matthew?' she murmured softly.

There was a stillness in the room. No moon. No stars glinting in the sky outside her window, lightening the inky darkness. Not a whisper of wind stirring the sea down in the cove.

A total silence.

Lauren held her breath. Waiting.

'Matthew,' she said again.

With a soft slither, one bundle of letters slipped to the floor from the foot of the bed. The sound made her jump. Her eyes penetrated the gloom, her body taut, her fingers gripping the linen sheet that covered her.

'Why, Matthew?' she whispered into the night. 'Why didn't you write to her anymore? Why did you leave her waiting like that? Why, Matthew?'

She could smell lavender scenting the bedclothes, and ... something else. A strange elusive aroma she couldn't at first define. It perplexed her, and then she realised.

The sea. The soft, salt tang of the sea.

But the voice didn't return.

★   ★   ★

'Can we stop and see the kittens?' Amy pleaded when they walked down to the little granite-built school the next morning. 'Adam leaves them in the garden in a basket with their mother. He won't mind.'

'Mr Poldean,' Lauren instructed. 'You mustn't call him Adam.'

'You do.'

'That's different, sweetheart. Adam's not my schoolteacher. He couldn't have all the children calling him by his first name, could he? Now remember — Mr Poldean.'

Her glance slid towards the thatched cottage as they passed. A quiver of a breeze coming in from the sea stirred the rounded pink heads of thrift growing in cracks of the grey stone wall, and her artist's eye wanted to capture the delicate picture they made. Would Adam mind if she did?

She knew, when they reached the playground, that she would see him surrounded by a chattering cluster of small children, like Gulliver and the Lilliputians. And Amy would be gone in a flash of speed, drawn to his side as if by a magnet. Adoring him, as they did.

'He has that effect on all females.' Those were Kate's words. But now Lauren wondered exactly what his sister-in-law had meant. He doesn't appear to have a girlfriend, she reflected, but surely a man as attractive as Adam must have someone in his life. Or had Kate's presence deterred such a relationship? If so, now that she had gone back to the States …

Once, when studying at university, he'd been engaged, Kate said. So what had happened? Had the woman married someone else? In their rush to catch the ferry back from St Michael's Mount, Kate had never finished telling her.

'Can I go to see the kittens, Mummy?'

'Another time, sweetheart. You'll be late for nursery school. Maybe, on the way home.'

And I can see Adam too, Lauren silently added, her heartbeat quickening at the thought.

★ ★ ★

Mr Quin had more or less taken over the house, rewiring and checking out the electrics, for the past few days. He muttered dreadfully at the state of it all, shaking his bald head in horror and thoroughly alarming Lauren.

'Proper death-trap you be living in, m'dear. No good fixing up these new appliances you've been delivered. Blow the place to kingdom come, they could. And these walls will need patching up with a bit of plaster here and there, then a nice coat of emulsion when I'm through. Like me to do that for you as well?'

Lauren agreed, but until he'd finished it was still the kitchen range and water heated in the copper. Luckily the weather had changed with the new month, and they basked in a mini-heatwave.

'Coming in like that at this time of year, 'tis far too early,' Ted Quin told her, chipping away at the wall beside the front door as he spoke. 'Won't last.'

Taking advantage of the warm spell, and to be out of his way, Lauren spent hours tidying the garden, discovering plants she'd never known existed before. When that was finished, she took her watercolours and went down to the beach. It was months since she'd done any painting. Moving in with Liz and her family after the divorce, there hadn't been either the time or space.

She studied the cove thoughtfully, taking in the position of the sun in relation to the cliff and the shadows that would be cast, before selecting a place well away from the incoming tide. Seascapes weren't something she'd tried before. Maybe she should visit the galleries Adam had suggested in St Ives to see exactly the type of picture that would sell.

The watercolour she'd completed of pink thrift on the grey stone wall had pleased her, and when he saw it Adam wanted to buy it to hang in his dining room.

'No way! I wouldn't dream of selling it to you,' she said firmly. 'But you can have it in exchange for the two Sunday lunches Amy and I had with you, and for restoring that kitchen range to working order.'

'Make it three Sunday lunches and we'll call it a deal,' he replied with a grin. 'I'll expect you and Amy this Sunday, and we'll have a ceremonial hanging of the painting.'

Adam was an enigma to her. From the kitchen window she frequently saw him fishing from his boat, or from the rocks bordering the cove. His long, lean body, silhouetted against the morning or evening sun, moved rhythmically as he swung out the line. And she found herself waiting in anticipation for him to be there.

She glanced down at the paper pinned to her easel and saw she was painting that scene. The rocks. The curve of the bay. The waves curling in across the sand.

An abundance of different pictures flooded through her mind. Evening, with the sun sinking below the rim of the sea, its rays stretching like crimson fingers across the limpid surface. Or maybe the coming of night, with Adam etched there on velvet rocks, a crescent moon silvering the sky.

The cove held so many possibilities. Every day was different. The sky never the same blue. The sea constantly changing — now calm; now raging in, white-flecked, to surge up the shore. Even the colour of the sand could alter — grey when wet from the receding tide; bleached pale gold by sunshine; ghostly at dusk.

Her brush flew over the paper, filling it with colour. The billowing white sails of a yacht appeared from behind the jutting cliff, and were instantly incorporated in the scene.

Did Aunt Hilda know about my artwork? she wondered. Was this the reason for such a legacy? She, too, Adam said, had been an artist. Little watercolours adorned the plain white walls of the cottage, and Lauren, recognising the scenery, was amazed by their excellence.

Her brush paused, leaving a deepening

spot of colour. And once again she asked herself, *Why did she choose me?*

* * *

'How about that trip over to St Ives on Saturday?' Adam's words surprised Lauren when they met at the school gate, as she collected Amy. 'You wanted to visit some of the art galleries there, didn't you? Or even the Tate. And I know a lovely little place for lunch, tucked away in a tiny courtyard.'

'Aren't Saturdays your day of rest from all the children?'

He lifted a quizzical eyebrow. 'Well, you're definitely not one — and as for Amy ...' he said, sitting down on his heels beside her, 'you're only an infant, aren't you?'

Wrinkling her forehead, the little girl looked up at Lauren. 'Am I, Mummy?'

'I think Mr Poldean is teasing you, sweetheart.' Lauren smiled at Adam. 'I'll ... we'll look forward to that. Thank you.'

It's just a visit to some art galleries,

she kept telling herself over the next couple of days, but the thought of spending a whole day with Adam filled her with excitement. As for what to wear, Lauren sifted through her very limited collection of clothes before deciding on the sleeveless white top and blue cotton skirt she'd worn for their first Sunday lunch.

She'd never seen Adam driving a car, so was surprised when he arrived in a low, open-topped, very ancient MG, and carefully lifted Amy into the narrow rear seat, where he'd fitted a booster one for her.

'If it's not too draughty for you, I'll leave the roof down, shall I? It's such a glorious day.'

To start with, their route was the same as when Lauren had driven Kate over to Penzance, and she pointed out St Michael's Mount to Amy as they passed.

'Is it a magic castle, with giants and witches and dragons?'

'There was a giant named Cormoran living there a long, long time ago, Amy,'

Adam said, slowing the car so that she could look across the bay. 'But a boy called Jack dug a big hole and then blew his trumpet to wake up the giant, who ran down the Mount to catch him, and fell into the hole.'

'Did he die, or does he still live there?'

'Oh, he died all right. And if you climb up the steep path to the castle, you can see a stone shaped like a heart that's said to be Cormoran's.'

'Can we go and see it, please?'

'Another day, maybe.'

The road branched off inland, and eventually they were driving into a large car park above St Ives, with the harbour and sea stretched out below them.

'Are we going on that little bus over there, or have we got to walk down that very, very steep hill?' Amy demanded, her voice high with excitement. 'I like buses.'

'Then we'll use that, shall we?' Adam said, helping her up the step into it.

He's got so much patience, Lauren thought. *Even though he's with children all day, every day.*

'OK,' he said, handing Lauren a leaflet once they climbed out in the middle of the town. 'This is a local street guide.'

He leaned over her shoulder, his chin almost resting on top of her head, one arm either side of her as he held the map, and she tried to keep her breathing steady.

'We're here. Most of the galleries are along there, and the Tate is there. It's almost ten o'clock, so Amy and I will meet you at midday outside the restaurant just there.' He pointed to a symbol on the map. 'You can have a quiet browse round and see what the galleries have to offer, while ...' He smiled down at the little girl clinging to his hand. 'While we go and explore the beaches and maybe see what the ice-cream shop has to offer.'

'Are you sure you don't mind?' Lauren said doubtfully, taking the guide from him.

'Would I be here if I did? Off you go now, or Amy and I won't have enough time to eat our ice-creams before it's lunch.'

Lauren watched as they walked away down the hill to the harbour, the tall man bending slightly sideways and her diminutive daughter gazing up at him, chattering nonstop. Then, with a glance at the street map, she went to find the galleries.

Within minutes she was lost in a melee of different styles, some garish with colour, others soft and muted; oils, watercolours, pastels, sketches, pen and ink, abstract or minutely detailed — all filling her with inspiration and challenge.

When she walked along the harbour-side to find the road leading up to the Tate, she saw on the sands a small figure patting out a castle from a red bucket and realised it was Amy, with Adam kneeling beside her carefully arranging stones, or maybe shells, around a second one. Amy, she noticed, was giving instructions as to their exact location.

Resting on his heels, Adam looked across and raised one hand, then indicated to Amy where her mother was standing. Even at that distance, Lauren could see the wide beam of delight on her daughter's small face as she waved her bucket and spade, before turning back to continue her construction work.

Having found the curved white building of the Tate, Lauren decided it would take far too long to tour that, and be back at the restaurant by twelve o'clock, so vowed to do it another day when Amy was at nursery school. Leaning on a rail and gazing out to the bay, she marvelled at the clarity of the light, giving the sea and sky a sharp brilliance, and remembered that was the reason so many artists had lived here over the years.

For the first time in many weeks, she felt at peace, absorbing the surrounding tranquillity, her whole body completely relaxed. *This is where I want to be*, she thought contentedly. And into her mind drifted the image of Amy and Adam, together on the sands.

Promptly at midday, she was waiting in the courtyard of the tiny restaurant, gazing through its bow windows at round tables with wheel-back chairs drawn up against them. A menu for the day was attached to the outside wall, and she read it in eager anticipation, deciding what she would eat.

A shriek from behind soon told her that Amy had arrived, swinging her new red bucket and yellow spade in one hand, while the other clung to Adam's. 'I made trillions of sand castles, Mummy, and Adam dug a moat, and it was right down to the sea, and all the water came rushing in with the waves, and it went all round my castles, and Adam said it was just like St Michael's Mount, and he found a funny-shaped stone and we pretended it was the giant, and I buried him in the sand, like that boy Jack did — didn't I, Adam?'

'Mr Poldean, Amy! You mustn't call him Adam.'

'But he *is* Adam, aren't you?'

'How about finding a table for lunch, Amy?' he suggested, adroitly changing the subject — which, Lauren decided, he seemed to be very good at doing.

'Let's have this one by the window,'

Amy said, clambering onto a chair. 'Then we can see all the people going past, and I can wave to them, and then they might come in and have some lunch as well, and the waitress ladies will be very pleased, won't they, 'cause they'll have lots and lots of money.'

'Did the galleries produce any inspiration, Lauren?' Adam asked, sitting down and passing the menu to her.

'Lots, but there's no way my work is as good as what's on show there — and it never will be,' she said ruefully.

'Lauren! Don't put yourself down. That watercolour of my garden wall with all the pink thrift is perfect. Just as good, if not better, than many I've seen for sale in the galleries round here. You've definitely got talent — like your great-aunt. It must run in the family. Now,' he said, scanning the menu, 'I can thoroughly recommend the cauliflower and stilton soup, and their smoked mackerel salad has a dressing that's a secret recipe even Mrs Quin doesn't know, while the strawberry roulade is out of this world.'

'All of it, please,' Amy said eagerly.

'Amy! You'll never eat all that,' Lauren said.

'But I'm very, very hungry, Mummy. Adam said it's the sea air — it gives you an appetite. Didn't you, Adam?'

He laughed and nodded his head. 'You're quite right, Amy. That's exactly what I said, but that was before you had an enormous honey and ginger ice-cream cornet. Shall we ask if they can do a special-sized portion?'

'Yes, please, Adam, 'cause that would leave room for another ice-cream this afternoon, wouldn't it?'

Lauren leaned her back against the cushion of the chair, feeling the warmth of the sun through the window as she drank her coffee at the end of their meal. The sound of voices from others filling the restaurant merged into the background. It was as though there were just the three of them, together in a small bubble of time — and she wanted to it to stay like that forever.

'Mummy told Aunty Liz that nobody

124

wants us,' Amy's voice filtered through her thoughts. 'And Aunty Liz said that was very sad, but somebody would want us, one day.' The little girl gave a big sigh. 'I do keep wishing, but it's taking that magic boat a very, very long time.'

Picking up her spoon, she trailed it through the strawberry juice left in her glass bowl. Then her cheeks dimpled into a smile and she looked up at Adam with wide eyes. 'Does nobody want you, Adam? 'Cause if they don't, we could have you, couldn't we, Mummy? And then all of us would be wanted, wouldn't we?'

Feeling heat burn in her cheeks that definitely didn't come from the sunshine, Lauren bent to find her handbag, and quickly stood up. 'That was a lovely lunch, Adam. My treat, so I'll go and get the bill.'

'No way ... ' he began, but she interrupted him, saying, 'All those Sunday lunches ... Now it's my turn.' She hurried across to the counter before he could protest any more.

Standing there and waiting while the waitress printed out the bill, Lauren idly watched groups of people meander down the cobbled street: families trailing small children and buggies; teenagers laughing together as they bit into hot pasties; those who were aged, walking wearily in the heat. The chatter of different voices rose and fell. Footsteps clattered. A wasp droned against the window, trying to escape.

'There you are, madam.' The waitress was handing her the bill, but Lauren's gaze was fixed on those passing by outside.

It couldn't be. She knew it couldn't be. The room swirled round her, as her whitening fingers gripped the edge of the counter.

There was no way that the man already disappearing round a bend in the narrow street could be Duncan. No way at all.

'Are you all right, Lauren?' Adam's voice behind her was concerned.

'I'm fine,' she replied, handing her

bank card to the waitress. 'It's just a bit ... hot ... in here, that's all.'

It wasn't Duncan. Of course; she knew that. Just someone similar. And from a distance ...

But her pleasure in the day was gone.

9

Now that she'd started painting again, Lauren found it difficult to stop. Her enthusiasm grew, and she saw potential pictures all around her.

It was nearly eight o'clock on a perfect June evening. Amy was asleep. The novelty of nursery school and days in the fresh air meant that Lauren had no problem persuading her to go to bed. She was tired out.

A smell of emulsion permeated the living room, its furniture piled into the centre, waiting for Mr Quin to resume work next morning. Lauren couldn't sit in there to read, so she took her book out to the wooden seat among the lavender and roses below the kitchen window.

One magnificent bloom caught her eye — a delicate shade of peach blending into a deep orange centre. Tomorrow it would be full-blown, ready to shed its petals.

Over. Darting back indoors, Lauren came out with her box of watercolours, eager to capture its perfection before the daylight faded.

'Absolutely beautiful.'

Adam's voice came softly, breaking her concentration. So engrossed was she that she hadn't heard, or seen, him climb the steps from the beach where he'd been fishing, but now his shadow stretched across the garden from where he stood.

Lauren smiled, dipping her brush into a jar of water before taking up more colour. 'It is, isn't it,' she replied, then realised he wasn't looking at the painting. His gaze was fixed on her. Heat fired into her cheeks and she bent her head, hiding her face in golden wings of hair, fixing her eyes on the final petal as she outlined its edge.

'Will it disturb your concentration if I stay here and watch?'

'No,' she said, not daring to look at him.

She heard the brush of cloth against wood as he lowered himself onto the seat beside her, and breathed in a mixture of sea salt and spice clinging to his skin. Warmth radiated from his body to envelop hers.

He sat, silent, but she was acutely conscious that he followed every movement of her hand as the brush travelled. A blackbird flew down from the hedge, probing the lawn with its beak. Then, with a quick flutter of sooty wings, it alighted on the top of her easel, head bent as if to study the image she was creating.

'Praise indeed!' Adam murmured, and the words feathered the lobe of her ear, sending a pulse of delight winging through her.

Abruptly she stood up, frightening the bird who, with an indignant shrill of alarm, returned to its nest in the hedge.

'It's getting too dark,' she stammered.

'I'll carry that inside for you.'

Their hands met on the rim of the easel, and hers jerked away as if burned, water slopping from the jar to soak into her jeans. Hastily, she stepped back and went into the house.

'Ted Quin's done a good job in here.'

130

Adam's eyes scanned the room as he followed Lauren through the doorway of the kitchen. 'And everything's in working order now.' He nodded in the direction of the gleaming cooker and fridge. 'Has he sorted out the hot water yet?'

Lauren reached for the kettle and filled it from the tap, then turned on the second one, sending a stream scalding into the sink.

Adam grinned. 'That must make a difference.'

'He works like a Trojan. Here at the crack of dawn, not even stopping for a bite to eat midday, although he does make up for that with endless mugs of very strong tea.'

'That's why all his hair fell out,' Adam said dryly.

'From drinking tea?' Lauren gasped, staring down at the caddy with horror. Then she saw his lips curve as he began to laugh. 'Are you going to risk a cup, or would you feel safer with coffee?'

'After all that, it'd better be coffee.' He picked up the jar and was spooning granules into two mugs, before he put down the spoon and looked ruefully at her. 'Sorry! I rather got into the habit of making a hot drink for your great-aunt whenever I came up here in the evenings.'

Lauren poured in boiling water and added milk. 'Tell me about her,' she said, leading the way back out to the garden seat.

The sun had sunk below the horizon, bordering it with scarlet that melted away into pink-suffused clouds above. One lone star winked in the distance.

'Do you mind sitting out here?' she asked.

'It's much too beautiful an evening to waste,' he replied, leaning back on the wooden seat and balancing his mug on its armrest. 'That rose has changed already, you know. Just in a matter of a few minutes.'

'And by this time tomorrow, all the petals will have fallen,' she said regretfully.

'But now you've made it immortal. Never to fade. Always to retain its perfection.'

'I suppose I have.' She smiled content-edly. 'Now, tell me about Aunt Hilda.'

'What do you want to know about her?'

'What she was like. It seems strange to me that in this day and age someone could become reclusive like that. There must have been a reason.'

'Maybe there was,' he said quietly.

Remembering the letters, Lauren asked, 'What was your grandfather's name?'

He looked puzzled. 'My grandfather?'

'Yours is a Cornish family?' she persisted.

'Yes,' he said slowly. 'My father was born over near Sennen Cove. Not all that far away. His parents — my grandparents — were Mary and William Poldean.'

'William?' She echoed the name.

'William,' he repeated.

'Not Matthew?'

'Definitely William. It was my father's name, too. And it's my brother Daniel's second name. What made you ask about Matthew?'

'Was there one?' she enquired hopefully.

'My grandfather had several brothers

and sisters and a host of cousins. People did in those days.'

'Was one of them called Matthew?'

'I honestly don't know. Why is it so important?'

The sun had vanished now, leaving only a faint glow in the sky. Myriad stars glittered and danced over the sea. A line of white breakers was all that Lauren could see to show where it reached the shore. Her conscience troubled her. She wanted to confide in Adam, but the letters were Aunt Hilda's secrets, not meant to be revealed to anyone.

But Adam isn't just anyone, is he? she reasoned. *He was Aunt Hilda's closest, maybe only, friend.*

'I found some letters,' she admitted reluctantly. 'Love letters. To my great-aunt from someone called Matthew Poldean. I thought ... '

Adam picked up his mug of coffee and drained it, before replacing it on the arm of the seat. His face was only a pale outline in the twilight as he turned his head. 'You thought he might be my grandfather?' He was silent for a moment or two. 'There's a family Bible at my cottage. Everyone's birth and death is recorded in that. It was the kind of record people kept in days gone by, so if Matthew was one of the family, he's sure to be listed.'

The garden was very quiet. Even the sound of sea was muted; there was just the soft rasp of waves dragging at the shingle. In the growing dusk, Lauren could no longer determine where horizon and night sky met. She was conscious of Adam sitting there beside her, his head still turned in her direction. The distance between them seemed to be lessening, but she didn't move away.

One gentle finger tilted her chin, raising her face. His lips brushed lightly across her cheek until they reached the corner of her waiting mouth, and paused there. The thud of her heart drummed in her ears and her breathing quickened. Then her hands slid up to his shoulders, round to the base of his neck, and tangled into the thick silk of his hair. And only then did his mouth take possession of hers, sweeping her away in a rising crescendo of delight.

They remained quite still after the kiss ended, Adam's forehead resting on hers. Then, abruptly, he released her. 'That was unfair of me.'

'Unfair?' she echoed, opening her eyes to gaze up at the pale shape that was his face, silhouetted against the wall behind him. She tasted salt on her lips as her tongue ran over them. Salt from the sea spray that had feathered his skin.

'Unfair,' he repeated harshly, and stood up, shivering the leaves of lavender and lemon balm into fragrance as he strode rapidly back into the house.

His abruptness dismayed her. Had the eager response in her kiss horrified him? And yet, it was he who had made the first move. Or did he? she wondered. She had been drawn to him like metal to a magnet, swept into a force field, unable to hold back.

She heard the clatter of china in the sink and guessed he was washing their mugs, but she couldn't go indoors to face him and read condemnation in his eyes when he looked at her again. Here in the garden, it was dark, and here she would stay until he left.

His return took her by surprise. 'I'll let you know if I trace that name, Lauren.' His tone was distant, without its usual warmth.

For a moment she couldn't think what he was talking about, but then she re-membered. Matthew. Matthew Poldean. Somehow, now, it didn't matter anymore. Nothing mattered, except the rift growing between them.

'Adam.' Her voice held a plea. *Tell me what I've done*, she wanted to ask, but the words wouldn't force themselves through the tightness of her throat.

'Goodnight, Lauren. Thank you for the coffee.'

She sat huddled on the seat, her arms clenched round her body, head bent, listening for the click of the front door when he closed it. And as she went back into the kitchen, her hand brushed against the rose, scattering its wilting petals over the moonlit grass.

She couldn't sleep, her mind roving over that brief interlude in the garden, trying to determine what went wrong. *I enjoyed kissing him, and being kissed by him. Too much so, perhaps. Was that the reason?* A kiss between two friends, that's all it was.

But she knew it was much more than that. And it troubled her.

She lay, bedcovers pulled close to her chin, waiting; listening for the comforting voice to fill the room. But there was only silence.

Somewhere there was a moon. It brightened the room, gleaming on one polished post of the bed, illuminating the intricate carving. If it could make a piece of wood glow like that, what would it do to the glass galleon? Lauren wondered.

Her feet touched the floor, her toes curling away from its coldness after the warmth of the bed as she crept across the boards and out of the door. She'd forgotten the piled furniture in the living room. When eventually she reached it, the windowsill was bare. Where had Mr Quin put the delicate little ship? In the moonlight, her eyes scanned the room, panic growing when she switched on the lamp but still couldn't find it. Every surface in the room was bare.

As a last resort, she opened the bureau — and there it was, carefully wrapped in a piece of bubble plastic. Her fingers peeled it away; and, turning off the lamp, she went across the room to place the galleon in a pool of moonlight on the windowsill.

At first, she was disappointed. Without the powerful rays of the sun, the effect was nothing. No rainbows shimmering. No brilliant dazzle of colour. No myriad twinkling stars. And then she observed it more closely.

The whole ship glowed as if lit from within, like a pale, iridescent pearl. Each sail appeared to billow against the darkness of the night outside the window.

A ghost ship.

With a sense of foreboding, Lauren picked it up, the delicate strands of glass cold to her touch as she wrapped it again in its plastic shroud and returned it to the bureau.

*   *   *

Ted Quin drank his tea with her the following morning, an unusual thing for him to do. 'Half an hour 'til that first wall's completely dry, before I can get started on a second coat,' he explained, wiping his hands on a bit of rag when Lauren took a mug into the living room for him. 'Don't want to stir up no dust or 'twill be the devil to clean off again.'

'Then come and drink this while I'm working in the kitchen,' she suggested. 'I'd like some advice about the washing machine. It travels across the floor when it spins the clothes at the end of a cycle.'

'Vibration, that'll be,' he replied, nodding his head. 'And your floor do slope a bit. Some padding under one of they little feet most likely will cure that. I'll find a scrap of wood. Plenty down in my workshop. I'll bring it up with me tomorrow.'

Lauren opened a tin and offered him a chocolate biscuit, watching his roughened hand hesitate over the tempting selection before choosing one. 'Whole place is looking a mite better now,' he observed, biting into it.

'Thanks to you, Mr Quin,' Lauren replied, refilling his empty mug.

He took a deep draught and finished off the biscuit. 'Pity old Miss Trevaunance let it get so bad. Many's the time my wife told her she'd come up and give her a hand, but Miss Trevaunance were an independent old biddy — if you'll excuse the expression — 'specially near the end.'

Lauren held out the biscuit tin and waited again while he made his choice.

'Surprised us all when you and your little maid turned up — never having seen you down this way before. Big surprise, that was. All us thought she'd leave everything to young Adam Poldean. Took very kindly to him, did Miss Trevaunance.'

'It came as a surprise to me, too,' Lauren admitted. 'I didn't know my

141

great-aunt, you see. I still can't understand why she left it to me.'

He put down his mug. 'Blood's thicker
than water, they do say,' he muttered,
wiping the back of his hand across his
mouth, with a rasp of stubble. ''Twas
strange, though. A sort of kinship, they
had. Young Adam and the old lady. Both
losing their loved ones to the sea like that,
I suppose.' He pulled a paint-speckled old
tweed cap from the pocket of his overalls
and slapped it over his bald head as he
spoke. 'Best be getting back in there,
m'dear. That wall'll be ready by now.'

Lauren caught his sleeve, her curiosity
aroused. 'Both losing their loved ones,' she
repeated. 'What do you mean, Mr Quin?'

'Miss Trevaunance and young Adam
Poldean,' he said. 'Lost their sweethearts
by drowning out there.' He nodded his
head in the direction of the sea. 'Drew
them together, I daresay. Her knowing the
pain he was suffering. And Adam glad to
have someone to confide in.'

He edged himself through the kitchen
doorway and across the hall. Lauren

followed closely, needing to know more. 'But when did all this happen, Mr Quin?'

Pushing open the living room door, he picked up his roller and tray. 'I remember my mother talking, though I was only a scrap of a youngster then. Big ears children have, don't they, m'dear, when it's something they're not supposed to be hearing? I daresay your little maid's just the same.'

Lauren held back her impatience. 'My great-aunt, Mr Quin — what happened?'

'Mind this don't splash on you.' Mr Quin climbed up a pair of steps and dragged the roller across the wall. 'Engaged to be married, she was, Miss Trevaunance. Fellow from over Sennen way. He'd been crippled in the war. I recall my mother saying that did help him drowning, only having one leg. Not that many fishermen can swim. Makes it a quicker end, so they do say.'

The roller dipped into the tray and back onto the wall again. 'And he was a fisherman, you see. Not much else he could do, I reckon. One of the crew on a

143

trawler. More of an industry round this way in those days. Died out a lot now. Too much competition from they foreign folk and all them government quotas, or whatever them's called. Killing off all our trade, they are.'

Lauren resisted the urge to hassle him on.

'Nasty coast, this one is, in a storm,' Mr Quin continued, lifting the step-ladder to move it further along. 'And out on the sea's the last place you want to be. All they rocks. Miss Trevaunance was never the same after that happened, my mother said. Cut herself off from they as would comfort her.'

'And Adam Poldean's fiancée?'

Mr Quin tipped more emulsion into the tray. 'Now I do remember her. Lovely girl, that one. Met her when he was up at university, did Adam. 'Twould have been maybe ten or more years ago, I suppose. Came down here on holiday, they did. Stayed in his mother's cottage. That thatched place he do live in now. Prefer slate for a roof, I do. No chance of catching afire with that, you see.'

Lauren perched herself on the window-sill to listen, feeling the sun hot on her back. 'What was his fiancée like?'

'Quite a wilful sort of girl, I reckon, from the way she behaved. Pretty one, though. Had quite a temper when things weren't going her way. And young Adam is a thinking man. Enjoys peace and quiet at times. You've probably seen him down in the cove, fishing.'

Oh yes, Lauren thought, suddenly rueful as that first unfortunate occasion came to mind.

'Well, his young lady friend objected to that. Wanted him out and about with her, not out there on his own. Decided on a spot of rivalry, I do reckon.'

Mr Quin deftly caught a trickle of paint with the roller as it threatened to reach the floor, then continued. 'Several lads there were, staying down here same time that summer. Surfers, some of them were. One of them was a flash sort, I recall. Big sporty green car and a speedboat he'd hired. She turned her eye on him; wanted to make young Adam jealous, I daresay.'

Lauren's mind was already leaping ahead, guessing the conclusion.

'Boat weren't meant for seas like those round this way. Pesky little thing, only fit for a river. It overturned way out. Found floating, the lad still clinging on. Too late for the poor girl by then.'

He stood back to study the finished wall, then bent to move the step-ladder round to the next one. 'Adam always called in on Miss Trevaunance when he was home for his holidays. One of the few she would consent to see.' He gave a little shrug of his shoulders. 'And after that, they seemed to form a bond. Always made welcome, was Adam.' Chuckling, he added, 'More than you could say for the rest of us. Now, if you don't mind, I'd like to do by that window where you're sitting. 'Tis a pity for you to be missing the sunshine outside.'

Taking that as a polite dismissal, Lauren left him to continue, and went into the garden to sit on the wooden seat. It was only a few hours before that she'd

146

been here with Adam. Her mouth still felt the impression of his kiss. It was a kiss she would never forget.

Waves swept strongly in over the sand, striking the rocks on the far side of the cove with such force that plumes of spray rose high, like drifting smoke. She could taste their salt on her lips, reminding her once more of Adam.

Her mind travelled on. Did he resemble his kinsman, Matthew Poldean? Did both possess eyes as blue as the sea on a summer's day? Was that the reason Aunt Hilda trusted and valued his friendship — his similarity to her beloved Matthew? Her great-aunt drawn and held, too, by the fact that both had lost the person they loved to the sea? So why didn't Aunt Hilda leave the house to Adam, the man who was her only true friend?

10

Leaving Mr Quin to his decorating, Lauren went later that morning to collect Amy from nursery school. The wind had grown fiercer as the day clouded over. Now as she walked down the hill it gusted round her, at times almost blowing her off her feet; and every blade of grass on the bank lay flat in its path.

The fury of the waves shook the ground, making the cliffs tremble, their onslaught thundering the spray-filled air and sending wisps of seaweed flying past. Lauren's hair streamed around her face, thin strands flailing her cheeks and whipping into her eyes, making them sting.

Each child came from the playground, breath snatched away, clothes flapping wildly, to seek refuge against their parent. Lauren took Amy's hand, hurrying her back up the hill.

'I don't like it, Mummy,' the little girl

wailed as they leaned into the wind.

'We'll be home in five minutes, sweetheart.'

It took far longer. Every step was an effort.

As they rounded the final bend of the lane, Lauren stopped, an ominous thread weaving its way through her body. A car was drawn in close to the hedge. A car she didn't recognise.

Mr Quin greeted her in the hallway, his weather-beaten face anxious. 'I hope I done right, m'dear. Come all the way down from London, he said. Couldn't leave him out there in weather like this, could I?'

Movement stirred behind him. A figure loomed out from the kitchen and Duncan stood there, smiling at her while he moved towards Amy, holding out a gift-wrapped box, tied with pink ribbon. 'Look what Daddy's brought you, Princess. Now, come and give me a kiss.'

Lauren instinctively gripped her daughter's hand, aware of Mr Quin's eyes watching. 'This is my ex-husband,' she explained, trying desperately to keep her voice on a level note.

'Well then, if 'tis all right with you, m'dear, I'll gather my things and be out of your way. Light's too bad to do any more.' He threw a doubtful look at Duncan. 'Unless you'd rather I stayed on a while.'

'No need to do that,' Duncan assured him. 'We've things to discuss, and I'm sure you'll want to get home before this storm gets any worse.'

'I'll be up in the morning to shift that furniture, m'dear. Room should be nicely dried out by then.'

With growing dread, Lauren's gaze followed Mr Quin while he shrugged on his old anorak and went out, closing the front door behind him, before she turned to Duncan. 'How did you find me?'

He laughed. 'Oh, it wasn't all that difficult, but shall we let Amy open her present first? I'm sure you're going to love it, Princess.'

With a quick glance up at her mother, the little girl ran forward to clasp the box, then knelt down on the floor to tear off the wrapping. Her face lit up into a wide smile as she pulled back the tissue paper and lifted out a frothy pink fairy dress, and under it, a pair of gossamer wings. 'Oh, Daddy! It's so beautiful. Can I go and put it on, Mummy?'

Swallowing hard, Lauren nodded, and the child ran up the stairs to her bedroom.

Leading the way into the kitchen, Lauren sank onto a chair, her legs shaking so much that she felt she was about to keel over, and repeated her question. 'How did you find me?'

'I went to see your friend Liz.'

Lauren glared at him. 'She didn't tell you. She would never do that.'

Sitting down opposite her, he laughed again. 'Oh, you can rest assured about that. However, while she was making some tea — and while we're about it, I wouldn't mind a cup now, darling — I read a postcard that was propped up on the mantelpiece.' Leaning forward, he fixed his gaze on her. 'Such a pretty picture of St Michael's Mount.

And on the back of it was how Amy had settled in at Porthvose nursery school, and how remote and dilapidated Aunt Hilda's house was, right on the cliff edge.'

With horror, Lauren remembered that day she and Kate were over on the island, and how she'd bought and sent that postcard. A sudden flurry of rain hit the window like pebbles on a drum, and a jag of lightning flooded the sky with brilliance, making her jump.

'It wasn't difficult to find the place on a map — and that old gossip in the village shop was only too pleased to tell me all about the young woman who'd inherited the old house up on the cliff.'

Going over to the sink to fill the kettle, Lauren was desperate to prevent Duncan from seeing her fear.

'Your great-aunt certainly did us a good turn. This place will be worth a fortune once it's done up a bit. Very desirable position, too. No problem selling it, with a view like that. Be snapped up in no time.'

'I've no intention of selling it,' Lauren replied tersely. 'It's our home now. Amy's and mine.'

'Not anymore, darling. You're both coming to New Zealand with me.'

'Both of us?' Her voice was full of sarcasm. 'And what does your new wife think about that?'

'Not her problem.'

Lauren dropped teabags into two mugs and poured on water, doing it automatically like a robot, then added milk from the fridge. 'A ménage a trois, is that what you intend?'

'Three of us, yes. You, me and Amy. A new life together. My new job with the law firm out there is fantastic — and so is the money.'

Frowning, Lauren asked slowly, 'Has Naomi left you already?'

His mouth twisted. 'The marriage was a mistake. OK, so I admit I acted badly. Naomi is a very sexy woman, and I lost my head. It happens. Only, now I've come to my senses again. It's you I love, Lauren. No one else.'

She stared back at him. *This is the man I shared my life with for seven years*, she reflected. *The man I adored. The father of my child. And yet, now he arouses nothing in me whatsoever. Not the slightest flicker of feeling. It's unbelievable. He could be a total stranger.*

Liz's words floated into her mind. *'He was never the right man for you.'*

'I'm sorry, Duncan. There's no way I'm ever coming back to you. I don't love you anymore.'

'But you must. You always did.' His voice was urgent.

'Once I did,' she said. 'But you destroyed that love, Duncan. And now it's gone forever.'

'Tomorrow you'll feel different.'

She shook her head. 'Not tomorrow, or any other day. Everything is over between us.' *As if it had never been*, she thought.

The room had darkened with the rain, and she reached out to switch on the light, revealing Duncan's bleak face. The desperation in his eyes filled her with sadness. *What will his life be like now?* she wondered. *Drifting from one relationship to the next, growing older, never finding what he wants. A sad and lonely man.*

'Look at me! Look at me!' Amy danced in through the door, a froth of pink tulle and glitter.

As the sky lit up with the next flash of lightning, thunder crashed overhead, and the lights went out, sending the little girl running to the safety of her mother's arms.

'I don't like it, Mummy!' she shrieked. 'Don't let it hurt me. Make it go away.'

'It's only a noise, sweetheart,' Lauren whispered, holding her close and kissing the top of her head. 'It can't hurt you.' But she wasn't convinced by her own words.

The full force of the storm hit the cove within minutes. Wind whistled, high-pitched, past the chimneys, and Lauren was terrified that any second one would crash down, scattering slates and rafters as it landed on top of them. There was no way Duncan could leave, and Lauren almost felt glad that she wasn't on her own with Amy in such frightening conditions. Lightning lit the whole sky, forking down to be lost in the rising waves. Rain streamed down the windowpanes, dripping rhythmically onto the wooden seat outside. A drainpipe rattled.

Lauren recalled Kate pointing out the line of seaweed where the cliff steps descended to the beach, and wondered just how far the water could rise when lashed by such fury. The rattle of the drainpipe intensified. Any second it would be torn away. And there was something else; a noise that repeated itself in a constant rhythm. It puzzled her, until she realised someone was knocking on the front door.

With Amy still clinging like a limpet to her, Lauren found her way into the darkened hall. As she tugged open the door, it nearly dragged her arms from their sockets as the gale swept it outwards.

'Lauren! Are you all right?'

Water streamed from Adam's hair, plastering it to his forehead as he stepped inside, fighting to close the door behind him. Lauren's skin shivered in the scatter of raindrops from his Barbour jacket when he turned. Her hand reached out impulsively to touch his cold wet cheek.

'A visitor, darling? In this weather?'

The hallway was lit by another flash of lightning, revealing Duncan standing behind her, and Lauren saw Adam's expression change.

11

'This is Duncan, my ex-husband. He's ...' Lauren's words came in a rush, her fingers slipping away from Adam's wet cheek.

'Then you won't need both of us here.'

There was a tone in Adam's voice she'd never heard before. His face, in the constant flickers of light, was like granite. Water dripped from his clothes, pooling round his feet.

'Oh, Adam, you're drenched. Come into the kitchen and get dry. With the power off from the storm, I shall have to use the range to boil the kettle. And I'll never get it going without your help.' Even as she spoke the words, Lauren realised what a stupid excuse it was.

'It's OK,' he said curtly. 'I'll sort myself out when I get back home. I just wanted to make sure —'

'So you're the reason.' Duncan's voice was bleak.

Adam's back stiffened. 'Reason?'

'For Lauren's reluctance to come back to me.'

'Of course he's not, Duncan,' she protested, feeling her cheeks burn.

'You could have fooled me, darling. How many men do you have racing up here in the middle of a storm like this to ensure you're OK? Or was that just an excuse? I'm surprised your boyfriend hasn't got his own key by now.'

'Not everyone has your morals, Duncan,' Lauren blazed.

'Calm down, darling. Not in front of our daughter, please. Shall we go back into the kitchen? I'm sure you've got candles somewhere.'

'I'll go,' Adam said. 'It's obvious you have a lot to discuss with your ex-husband.'

'No, Adam. It's Duncan who's leaving. We've said everything we have to say to each other. Besides, the storm's easing now. There's no need for him to stay any longer.'

'But darling —' Duncan protested.

'Say goodbye to Amy.' Her hand reached out to the latch of the door. 'And we won't be coming back to you. This is our home now. But don't worry, I'm sure you'll soon find someone else, if your new wife fails to return. It's something you excel at.'

★　★　★

'So what was all that about?' Adam asked, following Lauren along the hallway and into the kitchen.

'Duncan, you mean?'

The storm was beginning to move away now, with only occasional jags of lightning splintering the dark sky. Without any warning, the power came back on.

Amy raised her head from where it was buried into Lauren's shoulder and smiled across at Adam.

'Wow!' he said. 'And who's this beautiful fairy? I didn't know there were any fairies living in this house.'

160

'It's me, Adam. You know it is. You're just teasing me,' she chortled, all her previous fears forgotten. 'I'm going to take it off now and put it back into the box. Then tomorrow I can take it to show all the other children at nursery school.'

After she'd left the room, Adam raised one eyebrow in question as he looked at Lauren. 'Well?'

'Naomi, Duncan's new wife, has left him. He came here expecting me to leap back into his arms and fly off to New Zealand with him.'

'So why didn't you? From what Kate said, I thought you were still in love with him.' He paused while his gaze searched hers. 'That's why, when I kissed you … knowing that … I had to leave … I felt I was taking advantage of you.'

'I did love him … even when I first came here.' She lowered her head, letting wings of hair fall forward to conceal her face. 'But not anymore. I realised that quite a while ago. And knew for certain as soon as I saw him again.'

Adam's hand closed over hers, his

161

thumb smoothing across her palm. 'Then maybe, one day....' The unspoken question hung in the air.

'Maybe,' she murmured. 'One day.'

And found herself lost in the depths of his kiss. A kiss that lingered longer and far deeper than the one they'd shared in the garden.

When he finally, and reluctantly, released her, Adam said, 'You remember you asked me about Matthew Poldean?'

Her head jerked up, her eyes meeting his. 'You've traced him?'

'A cousin on my father's side of the family. Born 7th of February 1920. Died 12th October 1943 when his trawler went onto the rocks off Lizard Point in a storm, and all crew were lost. It's recorded in the family Bible just as I hoped it would be.' For a moment there was silence, before he continued. 'My ancestor was your great-aunt's fiancé.'

'I know.'

'You do?'

'Ted Quin told me yesterday. I fed him with chocolate biscuits and suddenly he became quite chatty. Wouldn't stop talking. And out came the whole story. He said you and Aunt Hilda were drawn together because of it.'

'What else did Ted say, Lauren?' Adam asked quietly.

She looked at the taut fingers enclosing hers. 'That your fiancée was drowned, too, which was why Aunt Hilda befriended you. You both shared the same kind of grief.'

The rain had steadied. Lauren could hear it brush against the windowpanes like soft wings, above the roar of surf. Every so often lightning still lit the sky, but the thunder only murmured now, far away in the distance. The storm had passed.

Silence hung between them like a thick curtain. Lauren didn't know what to say, fearing that she'd already said too much, and opened old wounds.

'It did form a bond, I suppose. Although she never mentioned it, your great-aunt must have known that Matthew was distantly related to me.

Perhaps that was the reason.'

'Tell me about your fiancée.'

'Joanne?' Adam gave a wry laugh. 'She was beautiful, vivacious, extremely desirable, and revelled in that fact. We were both at the same university.' He shrugged. 'I fell in love. Desperately. As one does at that age. First love is always overwhelming. I brought her here on holiday — and the whole place bored her to tears. To me it is, and always will be, a haven of peace. To Joanne, it was deadly dull. She complained there was nowhere to go. Nothing to do.' Frowning, he shook his head. 'I couldn't understand it. But then, Cornwall is in my blood. I couldn't survive anywhere else.' He gave Lauren a rueful look. 'Cornish folk are like that, you see. We have deep roots.' His mouth relaxed into a smile. 'Probably buried far down in the tin and copper mines where our ancestors worked out their lifetimes.'

'Which is why your brother wanted his child to be born here,' Lauren said. 'Even though he's living in the States. So that

164

he'd be Cornish, too.'

'Quite mad, aren't we?' Adam laughed, then his face became serious. 'It would never have worked out, marriage to Joanne. I realised that with hindsight. She would never have agreed to settle here. But then …' His gaze burned down into Lauren's. 'Everything's very different when you're in love, isn't it? You're carried along as though on a wave, never considering the logic of things.'

He picked up his mug of tea and swirled the contents before drinking them. 'I should've known. Joanne made it quite plain that she had no intention of sitting on a beach all day while I was fishing. But after a term of studying, I'm afraid all I wanted to do was relax and unwind. Joanne wanted more from life than that. I was totally boring and incredibly selfish, she said. And she was right; I *was* being unfair.'

'It was your holiday, too,' Lauren reminded him.

'That wasn't how Joanne saw it. Anyway, there was a group of guys staying down here, all very keen on water sports. Windsurfing, sailing, water-skiing, that sort of thing. One had a speedboat. Joanne went out with him in it. There was a force-eight gale blowing that day. Not one that amateurs should take on.'

Lauren's fingers closed over his fist as it clenched the edge of the table.

'They didn't come back,' he said flatly. 'One of the helicopters patrolling the coast saw their upturned craft, with the guy clinging to it. Two days later, Joanne's body was washed up out near Lizard Point.'

'I'm so sorry, Adam.'

'Your great-aunt came down to the cottage when she heard. After that, I visited her whenever I was staying here. Then my mother died of cancer shortly after I graduated, and I returned to the village to teach. I've been here ever since.' His eyes were filled with sadness when he looked across the table at her. 'So Joanne was quite right, wasn't she? Totally boring.'

'Or dedicated,' Lauren suggested.

He sighed. 'It'd be nice to think so. I

want to see the children here grow up to appreciate and understand their heritage. I want them to feel as I do, proud to be Cornish. Our history goes back a long way, you know.'

'So they're encouraged to be smugglers and wreckers?' Lauren asked, trying to lighten his sadness.

He smiled. 'No, but at least they'll understand the reasons why their ancestors were driven to do such things. You see, some were fishermen, but most were tin and copper miners, living on a wage so meagre that no one could survive, let alone bring up a family. It wasn't just the cargo they were after when the rocks out there claimed a vessel. Food was on board — provisions for the voyage. At least it prevented their wives and children from starving. And the ship's timbers they salvaged kept them warm in the winter months.'

'So they weren't as wicked as they're made out to be?'

'A few, perhaps, but for the majority it was a means to survive.'

The roar of the surf was hushed now in the cove. Lauren pushed herself away from the table and rose to her feet. 'Would you like to read the letters Matthew Poldean wrote?'

'Do you mind?'

'I'm sure Aunt Hilda wouldn't. Not when you meant so much to her. The living room is still in chaos, I'm afraid, until Ted Quin returns in the morning, but at least I can reach the bureau.'

*　*　*

Only the soft rustle of pages disturbed the quietness. Lauren studied Adam's face as he read, his dark lashes concealing any expression in his eyes.

'What a pity they were never able to marry,' he said regretfully, placing the final letter on top of the rest.

'To be loved so much ... no wonder his death affected her for the rest of her life,' Lauren murmured. 'But surely not enough to cut herself off from every-one.' She retied the ribbons and put the bundles into the drawer, but when she tried to close it, it refused to budge.

'Let me try,' Adam suggested. 'I think there's something blocking it. Yes, look, more letters are caught down the back.' He carefully withdrew another ribbon-tied bundle. 'These aren't written by Matthew, though.'

'That's my mother's writing,' Lauren whispered, taking them from him. 'Perhaps … when she sent those photos … '

A folded sheet of paper slipped out from under the ribbon and fell to the floor. Lauren stooped and picked it up, glancing at it curiously. Her forehead creased into a frown. 'It's a birth certificate,' she breathed, rapidly scanning the words written on it. 'My mother's birth certificate. I don't understand. This shows Aunt Hilda as her mother and … Matthew Poldean as the father. But Aunt Hilda's sister was my grandmother.' She raised a perplexed face to Adam and held the certificate out to him. He read through its contents, then bent his head to hers.

'Not so puzzling, really, Lauren. It explains a great deal. No wonder your great-aunt became reclusive. She was pregnant, unmarried, her fiancé dead. In the 1940s, having an illegitimate child made a woman an outcast. She obviously gave the baby to her married sister to bring up as her own child.'

'So that accounts for all the photographs. I was *her* grandchild.' She stared, wide-eyed, at Adam. 'Somehow my mother must have found out, or maybe was told the truth. The letters she wrote to Aunt Hilda — although I suppose I shouldn't call her that now — may make everything clear.'

'Then you'd better read them.' He pulled a dustcover from the sofa and sat her down, placing the bundle on her lap.

Her fingers hesitated. 'It seems such an invasion of privacy.'

'I'm sure your mother would've wanted you to know the truth.'

'Then why didn't she tell me?'

'Maybe it was to protect your great-aunt — sorry, your true grandmother's secret. The elderly can hold entirely different views from modern-day people. To a woman in her nineties, like Hilda Treavaunance, illegitimacy was, and always would be, a shameful thing. The shadow of it would hang over her right to the end of her life.'

Sunshine was flooding the room now, shining in from a sky where only a few dark clouds remained to hide, then reveal, its brightness. As Lauren began to read, she heard Adam catch his breath.

'Magical,' she heard him whisper, and turned her head.

The glass galleon stood once more on the windowsill, every tiny sail scintillating as it caught and held the soft brilliance of the sun. Against the raindrops still clustering on the windowpanes, it appeared to ride its own sea of waves.

'It was the last gift Matthew gave to your great-aunt,' Adam explained. 'An engagement present, she said. She treasured it.'

'Not quite the last gift,' Lauren murmured.

171

'No,' Adam agreed, his fingertips travelling lightly across her cheekbone, leaving a bewildering trail of pleasure. 'That was your mother ... and eventually ... you.'

Lauren caught his hand and stilled it, bewildered by the effect his touch had on her. She compelled her voice to remain steady as she said, 'It's always been a puzzle why Aunt Hilda left this house and its surrounding beauty to me, but now it all makes sense. You told me once, didn't you, that as a girl she was inspired to paint the glorious scenery around here. Do you think, when my mother told her that art was going to be my career, she wanted to bequeath her own inspiration to me?'

'It wouldn't surprise me,' Adam replied, moving to sit beside her on the sofa. 'She never stopped talking about you towards the end; constantly turning the pages of those photograph albums whenever I came here. And gradually her world grew smaller, until only you and I filled it.'

172

He cupped Lauren's chin and tilted it so that her gaze was level with his. 'I think her final wish was that we should meet … and fall in love … as she and Matthew did.'

'But to live happily ever after,' Lauren murmured, mesmerised by the deep blue of his eyes.

His lips were too close for her to watch them form words, only feel them feather the corner of her mouth as he whispered, 'It wouldn't be too difficult to make that wish come true, would it, Lauren?'

'No,' she agreed softly. 'Not difficult at all.'

12

The wedding was to be in late September, when the hot summer was lazily drifting into a golden autumn. Most of the holidaymakers would have gone by then, leaving the beaches to quietness and peace again.

Lauren's paintings were changing, too. There were longer shadows on the sands, stretching away from the granite cliffs where the waves climbed higher, sending up a mist of spray as the wind increased in force.

Throughout the holiday season, many of her delicate watercolours had been sold in one of the smaller galleries in St Ives, bought by those who wanted to retain memories of leisurely days spent in the sunshine and the tranquillity of tiny coves, where the warm sea caressed the shore.

Amy, golden from hours playing in the

garden or paddling along the tide-line searching for shells and treasure, was to be bridesmaid. And Kate would be the matron of honour when she, Daniel and the baby, yet to be christened Richard Adam, returned to Cornwall at the beginning of that month. With Daniel's two years in America at an end, he was coming home to teach at the university again. This delighted Lauren, knowing she would soon be reunited with her friend. Over the intervening months, they'd kept in touch by Skype, and up to date with baby Richard's progress; but seeing them again would be entirely different.

One thing marred Lauren's happiness, however: a letter from Duncan, who was applying for joint custody of his daughter and requesting that she spend half the year in New Zealand with him and Sheila, his latest partner, whom he'd met there. They shared a beautiful home together, he wrote. Photos were enclosed. As Sheila was unable to have children, seeing his adored daughter on a regular basis would fulfil their life.

'Being a solicitor, he knows the procedure, Adam,' Lauren frantically told him. 'What am I going to do?'

'*We* will contest it together, Lauren. He can't win. Here, now, is Amy's home, with you and me.'

But the thought was there, all the time, as they made preparations for the wedding. And if Duncan did win, Amy might not even be with them on that special day.

★ ★ ★

One of the kittens had been chosen and was ready to leave its mother. With a new basket waiting, Lauren and Amy were having a picnic lunch with Adam under the trees in his garden.

'I shall call him Adam, like you,' Amy announced, stroking the kitten's soft fur.

'You've chosen a lady kitten, Amy,' he told her gently.

'Oh!'

'Do you want to swap it for a different

one?'

She frowned. 'No, I can't. I've told him he's going to be my very own. And I do like him the bestest.'

'Her, Amy,' Lauren said. 'You'll just have to think of another name, sweetheart.'

Kissing the top of the kitten's head, the little girl sighed. 'I wanted to call her Adam so much.' And then her mouth widened into a smile. 'I know! I'll call her Madam instead. It's nearly the same, isn't it?'

★   ★   ★

Another letter arrived from Duncan. Lauren opened it with trembling fingers. It said he was back in the UK for a short visit, and he was planning to come down to Cornwall that weekend so he could spend time with Amy. They needed to get to know each other again before he took her back to New Zealand, once his appeal was granted.

Today was Friday. Panic-stricken,

Lauren ran out into the garden, where Amy was teaching the kitten how to chase a toy mouse. 'A real mouse might creep into our house when we're asleep, Mummy, and nibble all our food,' she explained. 'So Madam has to learn how to catch it.'

'Take the kitten indoors and put her back in her basket. We're going to see Adam.'

Looking surprised by the sharpness of Lauren's voice, Amy asked, 'Are you cross, Mummy? I wasn't being naughty, was I?'

'Of course you weren't, sweetheart. But we need to hurry.'

Adam was sorting books, ready for his move to the house on the cliff after their marriage, but greeted them both with pleasure as they burst in through the door, his face becoming serious when he saw Lauren's distress. 'Go and tell the other kittens what Madam has been doing, Amy,' he suggested, guiding the little girl into the garden. When he returned, he said, 'Now, Lauren, what's

178

happened?'

Silently, she held out the letter for him to read.

'But that's tomorrow,' he commented. 'When Daniel, Kate and the baby arrive back home from the States.' He rubbed his chin thoughtfully for a moment. 'Their plane doesn't arrive until late in the evening, so they're stopping overnight near the airport. How about we go up there to meet them? I can use the school minibus, and bring us all back here on Sunday.' A teasing smile tilted his mouth at the corners. 'What a pity you and Amy won't be around for Duncan. At such short notice, he really can't expect you to cancel such an important event, can he?'

Lauren's breath sighed out with relief.

Adam's eyes scanned the letter again. 'Duncan hasn't given the address of where he's staying, or a phone number. How thoughtless of him. A solicitor, too. Not very efficient, is it? Probably imagined you'd just be sitting at home, waiting expectantly for him to arrive. Such a shame you can't let him know.'

'Adam! You're wicked!'

'Why's Adam wicked, Mummy? Has he been naughty?' Clutching two of the kittens, Amy ran into the room.

'Very naughty, sweetheart,' Lauren replied, giving the little girl a hug.

'Don't squash the kittens, Mummy.'

'We've got to go home, darling. Pack some clothes, and bring Madam down here to stay with the others.'

'Why?'

'Adam's taking us to London with him to meet Aunty Kate, Uncle Daniel and the baby.'

'Really and truly?'

'Really and truly, sweetheart. Come on, let's hurry.'

They were back within an hour.

'That was quick!' Adam said. 'I've arranged with Tom Quin to pop in and keep an eye on the kittens, and feed them when he takes his dog for a walk. He does that several times a day — to keep out of Mrs Quin's way, I think.'

★　★　★

Kate was surprised and delighted to find them waiting after the flight arrived. Hugging and kissing each one of them in turn, once, and then again, with tears streaming down her face, she exclaimed, 'I've missed you all so much! And I'm only crying because I'm so happy and excited to see you again. And this is Daniel, Lauren. I've told him so much about you — haven't I, darling? And about that horrible Duncan wanting to take away Amy.'

She bent down to give the little girl an extra kiss. 'And, would you believe it, Richard slept for nearly the entire flight. I was quite sure he'd scream throughout, and everyone would hate us, and none of the other passengers would be able to get any sleep. Have you sold any of those lovely watercolours, Lauren? Daniel absolutely adores the one you did of me and the baby — don't you, darling?'

Lauren smiled contentedly. Kate hadn't changed one bit, her mind still flitting from topic to topic, with hardly a pause for breath.

Amy was totally fascinated with baby Richard, leaning over his buggy to stroke his cheek, and laughing when he smiled at the touch of her hand.

'Can we have a baby, too, Mummy? One of our own to keep.'

* * *

It was very late on Sunday night when they arrived back in Porthvose. Both Amy and the baby were fast asleep, not even stirring when their mothers lifted them out of the minibus and carried them into Adam's cottage.

'I'd better get her home and into her own bed,' Lauren said, looking down at the sleeping child curled up on the sofa.

Adam put his hand on her arm. 'You'd better stay here tonight, Lauren. Just in case Duncan is still around. He's not going to be at all happy about you not being there.'

She hesitated. No way did she want to meet Duncan, guessing the sort of mood he'd be in. She remembered only too well his reaction when things didn't go his way.

'Kate, Daniel and the baby are sleeping in her old room,' Adam said. 'You and Amy can have my bed, and I'll sleep down here on the sofa. We're all tired after the excitement of seeing everyone again. Tomorrow I'll come up to the house with you, but I'm sure Duncan will be long gone.'

'Well ... '

'That's all sorted then. I'll go and make some tea while you take Amy upstairs. She can stay here with Kate when we go up to the house in the morning.'

* * *

Adam was right; there was no sign of Duncan. Lauren picked up the post from the mat inside the front door. The usual junk mail, plus one long white envelope. She felt her stomach contract as she opened it and saw the embossed name of the solicitor dealing with Amy's custody. As she unfolded the letter, its words blurred.

Silently, Adam took the sheet of paper from her trembling hand, his arm drawing her tense body close to his side. She waited for what seemed like an eternity as he read the contents. Then his arm tightened round her as he turned her to face him, and she saw he was smiling.

'It's all right, my darling. Listen to this: The father, divorced on the grounds of his adulterous way of life, who constantly changes his female partners, and lives abroad, can offer no permanent stability to this child. Removing her from her mother's loving care, no matter for how long or how short a time, would cause great distress and insecurity to the child. The mother is about to remarry and will be able to provide the child with a secure life and future. Therefore, no custody is granted to the father.'

'Oh, Adam!' Tears of relief slid down Lauren's cheeks, to be brushed away by his kiss.

* * *

Sunshine brightened the morning of their wedding with autumn gold. The whole village seemed to crowd into the tiny church, where the stone floor was patterned with rainbows of light coming in through the stained-glass windows. Every wooden pew had a tiny posy of white roses tied to its end, their delicate scent filling the air with sweetness.

Having no parents of her own, Lauren had asked Mr Quin to give her away. Stiffly, in his well-brushed dark suit, bald head gleaming, he stood in the porch, clutching her arm with a fierce grip.

Behind them was an excited Amy in a fairytale froth of pink tulle, chosen by herself, and a coronet of tiny rosebuds in her hair, to match those of her posy. Kate, regally tall in cerise silk, held the little girl's hand.

With a tremor of sound that vibrated up into the wooden rafters, the organ began to play, slightly wheezily at first, before gathering rhythm. Hymn sheets rustled, heads turned, and voices were hushed as Mr Quin and Lauren stepped together down the aisle, the honey-coloured silk of her dress whispering. As Adam moved into the aisle to greet her, Lauren was aware of nothing else but the depth of love filling his gaze, and she saw him smile.

Motes of dust danced on sunbeams as the solemn words of the marriage service echoed in the hollowness of the stone walls. Then voices rose in song, lifting up to be lost in the high arch of the roof.

The feast that followed went on for several hours. Mrs Quin even closed the shop for the whole day. Dancing continued until late at night.

Kate, Daniel and the baby were going to live in Adam's cottage now, and Amy was to stay with them for the weekend, much to her delight.

'Kittens *and* a baby,' she breathed, happily.

★　★　★

I love you, love you, love you.
The words pulsed in the air around the four-poster bed. It was a voice so familiar,

now, to Lauren. No longer unknown.

Love you, love you …

And finally, whispered away, to become part of Adam, as she did.

Other titles in the
Linford Romance Library:

SUMMER'S DREAM

Jean M. Long

Talented designer Juliet Croft is devastated when the company she works for closes. She takes a temporary job at the Linden Manor Hotel, but soon hears rumours that the business is in financial difficulties — and suspects that Sheldon's, a rival company, is involved. During her work, she renews her friendship with Scott, a former colleague. At the same time, she must cope with her growing feelings for Martin Glover, the hotel manager. Trouble is, he's already taken . . .

SEEING SHADOWS

Susan Udy

Lexie Brookes is busy running her hairdressing salon and wondering what to do about her cooling relationship with her partner, Danny. When the jewellery shop next door is broken into via her own premises, the owner — the wealthy and infuriatingly arrogant Bruno Cavendish — blames her for his losses. Then Danny disappears, and Lexie is suddenly targeted by a mysterious stalker. To add to the turmoil, Bruno appears to be attracted to her, and she finds herself equally drawn to him . . .

A DATE WITH ROMANCE

Toni Anders

Refusing to live in the shadow of her father, a famous TV chef, Lauren Tate runs her own cake shop with her best friend, Daisy. Having been unlucky in love, Lauren pours her energy into her business — until she meets her handsome new neighbour, Jake, who is keen to strike up a friendship with her. Will Lauren decide to take him up on the offer? Then Daisy has an accident, and announces she'll be following her partner to America once she has healed — leaving Lauren with some difficult choices . . .

ALL BECAUSE OF BAXTER

Sharon Booth

When Ellie's marriage unexpectedly ends, she and her young son Jacob seek refuge with Ellie's cousin Angie. But Angie soon tires of her house guests, including her own boisterous rescue dog, Baxter. When Baxter literally bumps into Dylan, Ellie dares to dream of a happy ending at last. But time is running out for them, and it seems Dylan has a secret that may jeopardise everything. Must Ellie give up on her dreams, or can Baxter save the day?

FESTIVAL FEVER

Margaret Mounsdon

Fleur Denman is given the chance of a lifetime to front the Ridgly Parva Arts and History Festival — but some locals have long memories, and aren't prepared to overlook the scandal that once blackened the Denman name. In the face of adversity, Fleur sets out to prove her worth. Then some festival money goes missing, and Ben Salt, the main sponsor, is among the first to point an accusing finger in her direction. To make matters worse, Fleur finds herself increasingly attracted to him . . .

HEART OF THE MOUNTAIN

Carol MacLean

Emotionally burned out from her job as a nurse, Beth leaves London for the Scottish Highlands and the peace of her aunt's cottage. Here she meets Alex, a man who is determined to live life to the full after the death of his fiancée in a climbing accident. Despite her wish for a quiet life, Beth is pulled into a friendship with Alex's sister, bubbly Sarah-Jayne, and finds herself increasingly drawn to Alex . . .